Acting Edition

A Very Sordid Wedding

by Del Shores

Song "Sordid Lives" by Margot Rose & Beverly Nero

I0589009

MUSIC AND THIRD-PARTY MATERIALS USE NOTE

IMPORTANT BILLING AND CREDIT REQUIREMENTS

A VERY SORDID WEDDING was originally commissioned and produced by Craig Lynch and Jeff Rane for Uptown Players at the Kalita Humphreys Theater in Dallas, Texas on September 24, 2021. The production was directed by Del Shores, assistant directed by Emerson Collins. The scenic design was by Dennis Canright, hair/wigs/makeup designed by Coy Covington and Michael Moore, costume design by Suzanne Cranford, assistant costume design by Breianna Barrington and Jordan Rodriguez. Prop design was by Jane Quetin, sound design by Brian Christensen, lighting design by Kyle Harris, tattoo design by Shelly Denning, photography by Mike Morgan, graphic design by Sherry Etzel, fight choreography by Robin Armstrong with additional music scored by Joe Patrick Ward. The stage manager was Renee Dessommes, the assistant stage managers/running crew were Harper Hadley, Britton Melton and Avery Davis. The cast, in alphabetical order was as follows:

ROGER/EDNA JEAN/CASHIER/
ANTI-EQUALITY SISTER . . . . Christopher Abraham
KYLE . . . . Branden A. Bailey
ODELL/JIMMY RAY . . . . Hunter Barnett
WILSON . . . . Bradley Campbell
SISSY . . . . Allyn Carrell
JUANITA/MRS. BARNES . . . . Mari Deese Hampton
WARDELL . . . . Steve Golin
MARTY/NURSE SAMPLE/TRAGIC DRAG QUEEN . . . . Kelly Groves
HARDY/PETER . . . . Israel J. Henry
GRETA . . . . Dom G. Jones
NOLETA . . . . Shannon McGrann/Cara Serber
G.W . . . . Bruce Melena
TY . . . . Kevin Moore
CASSIE NOVA . . . . James Love
LATRELLE . . . . Ivy Opdyke
LAVONDA . . . . Morgana Shaw
PEGGY/VERA/AUNT LITTLE NEECY/HORTENSE . . . . Sally Soldo
BROTHER BOY . . . . Paul J. Williams

and Emerson Collins as **BILLY JOE DOBSON**

ENSEMBLE . . . . Harper Hadley, Britton Melton
ADDITIONAL VOICES . . . . Ron Corning (Newscaster),
Matt Holmes (*Hoarders* Host), Renee Dessommes (Brenda),
Emerson Collins (Doctor/Brenda's Son), Del Shores (Rose Room
Announcer)

A Very Sordid Wedding
A play based on the Beard Collins Shores Production film
Produced by Emerson Collins and Del Shores.

Special thanks to those who made this production possible:
Jerre van den Bent, Tim Chase & Eric Powell, Brian Jansen.

CHARACTERS

WARDELL

G.W.

ODELL

LAVONDA

LATRELLE

SISSY

NOLETA

JUANITA

BROTHER BOY

PEGGY

HOARDERS HOST – (Voice over)

NEWCASTER – (Voice over)

BRENDA – (Voice over)

JIMMY RAY

ROGER

TY

KYLE

MRS. BARNES

AUNT LITTLE NEECY – (Off stage)

HORTENSE

NURSE SAMPLE

VERA

HARDY

BILLY JOE

MARTY

CASHIER

GRETA

WILSON

PETER

EDNA JEAN

CASSIE NOVA

ROSE ROOM ANNOUNCER – (Voice over)

TRAGIC DRAG QUEEN

SETTING

Various locations throughout Winters, Longview, and Dallas, Texas.

TIME

The play takes place over several days July 2015.

For
Emerson Collins

This play is dedicated to all who fought so hard for Equality

ACT ONE

Scene One

(Cast: **WARDELL, G.W., ODELL, LAVONDA, LATRELLE, SISSY, JUANITA, NOLETA, BROTHER BOY, PEGGY.***)*

(The sets are suggestions, very minimal. Quick furniture changes made by cast members/crew and creative ways to achieve them are suggested throughout the script. They are suggestions and can be adjusted to fit the needs of each stage and production. This play is based on the film by the same name. Although theatre, the play is designed to be fast-paced with lighting and set/scene changes and a strong acting troupe with multiple castings to accomplish a film style while still honoring theatre.)

(In darkness, a piano intro to a very gay version of [**"THE BRIDAL CHORUS"**] *fills the theatre. Oh yes, baby, it's a wedding! Lights up church.* **WARDELL,** *the good ol' senior cowboy groom, smiles in nervous anticipation. Standing by the groom are his groomsmen:* **ODELL, WARDELL***'s younger, dim-witted brother and* **G.W., WARDELL***'s best friend, who has two prosthetic legs. On the bride's side are the bridesmaids:* **LAVONDA,** *a flashy, mouthy redhead, the maid of*

1

honor, **LATRELLE**, **LAVONDA**'s *uptight sister and* **SISSY**, *their codependent aunt. They are all dressed in Tammy Wynette orange jumpsuits. A table (or coffin) with a "This Do In Remembrance of Me" cloth over it sits in front of the wedding party. A dramatic segue of* **["THE BRIDAL CHORUS"]** *brings lights up on the congregation/audience, which looks as if gay threw up, decorated with boas, rainbows and every gay cliché available. In the audience,* **JUANITA**, *this town's barfly, discreetly pops a beer and swigs as she stands while* **NOLETA**, **LAVONDA**'s *hot mess of a best friend, also stands.)*

NOLETA. *(Motions, to audience.)* Stand up, y'all! Stand up.

*(**BROTHER BOY**, an aging drag queen, appears at the entrance of the theatre, in a beautiful wedding gown, carrying a rainbow bouquet and swishes down the aisle.* **SISSY**, **LAVONDA** *and* **LATRELLE** *perform a little dance routine to* **["THE BRIDAL CHORUS"]** *as* **BROTHER BOY** *processes. Note: If theatre cannot accommodate actors being in audience, then director should stage wedding completely on the stage with wedding guest extras from available cast.)*

JUANITA. Oh, I think she's so pretty.

*(As **BROTHER BOY** reaches the stage, **NOLETA** motions for audience to sit (if they stand.) **BROTHER BOY** stops for a moment and fixates on* **WARDELL**, *who lovingly smiles at his "bride".)*

BROTHER BOY. *(Smitten.)* Wardell.

WARDELL. I love you.

(**BROTHER BOY** *continues his walk. Blackout. Note: During blackout, the cloth is pulled off the table or coffin and* **PEGGY** *quickly and discreetly enters and either lies on a table or opens the coffin lid and stands behind it as* **BROTHER BOY** *screams in the darkness and all exit. Lights up!* **PEGGY** *flies off the table – or slams the coffin lid closed. Yes,* **PEGGY INGRAM, BROTHER BOY**'s *dead mama has risen! She wears a conservative funeral dress and a mink stole. Nightmare music cue* as lines overlap chaotically.)*

PEGGY. Well, I guess you didn't think I was gonna make it, did you, Earl?!

(*She begins to chase* **BROTHER BOY** *around the table or coffin.*)

BROTHER BOY. Mama!!! Ahhhh! Oh, lord. Help me! Help me –!

PEGGY. You ruined my funeral!

BROTHER BOY. Mama, go away!

PEGGY. Now I'm ruining your unnatural wedding!

BROTHER BOY. AHHHHHHH!

PEGGY. And I'm taking you right back to the mental institution so Dr. Eve can finish dehomosexualizin' you!

(**PEGGY** *starts hitting him with the mink stole, now chasing him across stage.*)

BROTHER BOY. No, you can't. I won't go! NOOOOOO!!!!

(Lights go strobe-like, horror music heightens*. During the lighting chaos, **BROTHER BOY** *removes the veil and gets under the covers of his bed (to hide the wedding gown). Lights up* **BROTHER BOY***'s room. A bed, a nightstand with a princess phone and a Tammy Wynette picture on it, a rack of drag gowns and boas complete the décor.* **BROTHER BOY** *bolts up, waking up from his nightmare screaming. Breathing hard, he picks up Tammy's picture.)*

(Whimpering.) Tammy, make all the ugly in the world go away.

(Lights out **BROTHER BOY***'s room.)*

---

* A license to produce A VERY SORDID WEDDING does not include a performance license for any third-party or copyrighted music. Licensees should create an original composition or use music in the public domain. For further information, please see Music Use Note.

Scene Two

(*Cast:* **WARDELL, G.W., JUANITA, ODELL, LATRELLE, JIMMY RAY, SISSY, ROGER.**)

(*Spot hits* **WARDELL**, *guitar in hand. He strums and sings.*)

WARDELL. (*Singing, upbeat, country.*)
WHO'S TO JUDGE WHO'S A SAINT WHO'S A SINNER?
LORD, IT'S TOUGH ENOUGH TO TRUDGE FROM BRUNCH
TO DINNER.
WE SEEK THE LIGHT OF TRUTH, BETWEEN OUR WHITE
LIES,
AND SLEEP AWAY OUR YOUTH UNDER TATTLE-TALE SKIES.
NOW WHO'S TO SAY WHO'S A SINNER AND WHO'S A SAINT?
WHO'S TO SAY WHO YOU CAN LOVE AND WHO YOU
CAIN'T?
WELL, IT'S EASY FOR THE POT TO CALL THE KETTLE
BLACK.
THEY'RE JUST JEALOUS OF THOSE HOT AND LUSTY
SORDID LIVES THEY LACK.

> (*Lights up on Bubba's Bar, directly behind* **WARDELL**'s "stage". Simple. A bar with three stools and a shelf of liquor behind the bar. During **WARDELL**'s verse, **G.W.** enters, followed by **ODELL** (if not also playing **JIMMY RAY**) and **JUANITA. G.W.** pulls out some drum sticks, sits on a stool and starts drumming his prosthetic legs and singing backup as the chorus starts. **ODELL** settles on another stool, picks up an empty beer bottle and starts blowing his "instrument", pausing between blows to sing backup. **JUANITA** has a tambourine and adds her own musical touch and backup singing. **WARDELL** begins to stroll across the apron of the stage, singing right to the audience.*)

(Singing.)

AIN'T IT A BITCH.

G.W., ODELL, JUANITA. *(Yelling.)* Bitch.

WARDELL. *(Singing.)*
SORTIN' OUT OUR SORDID LIVES. IT'S A BITCH.

G.W., ODELL, JUANITA. *(Yelling.)* Bitch.

WARDELL. *(Singing.)* WHEN YOU COME TO REALIZE.

> *(Lights up bench. **LATRELLE** enters, dressed in a nice, casual suit, carrying a bouquet of flowers. She stands in front of a park bench, places the flowers in front of a tombstone then sits on the bench.)*

(Singing.)

WHEN YOU CRACK YOURSELF A BOX OF CRACKER JACK,
YOU CAN GET A REALLY SHITTY PRIZE.
IT'S A BITCH.

G.W., ODELL, JUANITA. *(Yelling.)* Bitch.

WARDELL. *(Singing.)*
SORTIN' OUT OUR SORDID LIVES.

> *(**JIMMY RAY BREWTON**, the charming, handsome new pastor of Southside Baptist Church, enters, rolling a church sign. Lights up on sign. **JIMMY RAY** kneels and finishes the final letters on the church sign which reads: THE SUPREME COURT IS NOT THE SUPREME BEING! He stands back looking at the sign with pride, then exits, satisfied.)*

(Singing.)

WE STRUGGLE COMIN' DOWN THE CHUTE TO TAKE OUR
FIRST BREATH,

AND WE STRUGGLE FOR ACCEPTANCE FROM OUR BIRTH
TO OUR DEATH.

> *(Lights up on **SISSY**'s house. A tacky sofa, an old TV facing the sofa, a coffee table and an armchair complete the décor. **SISSY** is sitting on the couch, cigarette dangling from her mouth, a Bible in one hand and a cup of coffee in the other, dressed in a sleeveless blouse and culottes. She reads the Bible while smoking.)*

(Singing.)

BUT THE LORD'S TOO BUSY TRYIN' TO KEEP THE WORLD
ON ITS FEET
HE AIN'T GOT TIME TO GIVE A SHIT ABOUT WHAT GOES
ON BETWEEN THE SHEETS.

> *(**ROGER**, the swishy town beautician, enters and walks "down the street", spots the church sign. He stops, reads the sign, which pisses him off. He flips off the sign, throws his arms up in the air and exits.)*

(Singing.)

AIN'T IT A BITCH.

G.W., ODELL, JUANITA. *(Yelling.)* Bitch!

WARDELL. *(Singing.)*
SORTIN' OUT OUR SORDID LIVES
IT'S A BITCH.

G.W., ODELL, JUANITA. *(Yelling.)* Bitch!

WARDELL. *(Singing.)*
WHEN YOU COME TO REALIZE
CRACK YOURSELF A BOX OF CRACKER JACK,
YOU CAN GET A REALLY SHITTY PRIZE,
IT'S A BITCH.

G.W., ODELL, JUANITA. *(Yelling.)* Bitch!

WARDELL. *(Singing, big finish.)*
     SORTIN' OUT OUR SORRY, LITTLE SORDID LIVES.

JUANITA. *(Hands to heavens.)* Amen! Praise Jesus!

     (Lights out Bubba's Bar.)

Scene Three

(Cast: **SISSY**, **HOARDER'S HOST** *(Voice over),* **LAVONDA**, **T.V. NEWSCASTER** *(Voice over),* **NOLETA**.*)*

(Lights up on **SISSY***'s house.* **SISSY** *puts down her Bible, shudders a bit, then picks up the TV remote on the coffee table, punches a button. The TV roars to life.)*

HOARDERS HOST. *(On TV.)* Because of the hoarding, Brenda has not let anyone in her house for over twenty-three years.

SISSY. Oh my word! *(Yelling.)* LaVonda get in here! You're not gonna believe this hoarder's house!

*(***LAVONDA** *enters, wearing a fabulous turquoise, Texas-style jumpsuit.* **SISSY** *mutes TV.)*

LAVONDA. I can't. I am late for my hospital visitation duties and I am taking Noleta with me to see her Mama. *(Exits, yelling out off stage "kitchen back door".)* Noleta! We gotta skidaddle!

NOLETA. *(Off stage.)* I can't find my ponytail!

LAVONDA. *(Re-entering with a cup of coffee.)* I wonder why.

SISSY. Brenda's house makes Noleta's trailer look tidy. Collects dolls 'cause her daughter drowned when Brenda was passed out drunk.

LAVONDA. Tragic. You know I am just glad to see you back in front of that TV. You've had your nose stuck in the Bible for the last few months. You done?

SISSY. Almost. I had to take a break. Revelations scares the dickens out of me. Barely slept last night.

LAVONDA. I do not know what possessed you to read the entire Bible cover to cover. I think I'd kill myself.

SISSY. Well, with Ty and Kyle flittin' from one state to another getting gay married, coupled with that Supreme Court decision and now what's going on down at the church house, I just needed to figure out some things for myself.

LAVONDA. Seems to me if David can have Bathsheba's husband killed in battle so he can marry that adulteratin' pregnant tramp to add to his shit-ton of other wives, our nephew can marry the one man that he loves.

SISSY. You're being too hard on Bathsheba. David used his position as king to have his way with her! Do not blame the victim! How is Noleta's mama?

LAVONDA. Tests still pending. They've narrowed it down to either stomach cancer or a severe case of ptomaine which she mighta gotten from her very own leftover tuna casserole which she left out all night.

SISSY. Ooooh. In this heat?!

LAVONDA. Then she ate it for breakfast.

SISSY. Hortense knows better than that! It's summer and who eats tuna casserole for breakfast?

LAVONDA. Hortense! *(Takes SISSY's purse and digs.)* Can I borrow a pack of cigarettes? I'm running low.

SISSY. Yes, but you pay me back this time! They are so high now, oughta make us all quit. I'm gonna pray Hortense has ptomaine instead of stomach cancer.

(**NOLETA** *rushes in.*)

NOLETA. I can't find my ponytail!

LAVONDA. You want to borrow one of my Raquel Welch wigs?

NOLETA. No, that's alright, I'll just re-think my look on my way over to visit Mama.

SISSY. You wouldn't have that problem if you would just choose a look and stick to it.

LAVONDA. That's right. *(Pats her hair.)* Me and Sissy's hair has stood still for decades.

> *(**SISSY** sees something on the TV, grabs the remote and un-mutes it.)*

SISSY. Shh, shh!

TV NEWSCASTER VOICE. *(On TV.)* We interrupt this program to bring you the very latest on a developing story. We have confirmed that convicted serial killer Billy Joe Dobson, known as the Hitchhiker Murderer, has escaped from the Huntsville Men's Correctional Facility.

SISSY. Sweet baby Jesus! He's that serial killer from over in Longview who picked up hitchhikers and killed them by conkin' 'em on the head with a sledge hammer he stole while working at a meat packing plant right over in Tyler.

NOLETA. *(Fixed on TV.)* He is so hot!

LAVONDA. I guess I won't be hitchhiking anytime soon or I'll end up in the graveyard.

NOLETA. I might.

> *(Lights out **SISSY**'s house.)*

Scene Four

(Cast: **LATRELLE.***)*

(Lights up on bench as **LATRELLE** *rises, walks over to her Mama's grave.)*

LATRELLE. Well, Mama, it's been seventeen years since you died. A day you caused so much chaos and all hell broke loose! My son came out as gay right in front of your coffin and is now legally married to a... *(Whispers.)* ... black man, thanks to the U.S. Supreme Court. I'll give you a moment to roll over in your grave. Oh mama, so much has happened. Wilson left me. Took my credit cards. My beautiful home. I had to move into a seventeen hundred square foot house back here in Winters, Texas where there's a constant parade of crazy dancing in the streets.

(Country music cue* as lights fade on bench.)

---

* A license to produce A VERY SORDID WEDDING does not include a performance license for any third-party or copyrighted music. Licensees should create an original composition or use music in the public domain. For further information, please see Music Use Note.

Scene Five

*(Cast: **WARDELL, ODELL, G.W., JUANITA.***)*

(Lights up on Bubba's Bar, where the music blares. We find **WARDELL** behind the bar, **ODELL** and **G.W.** perched on their stools, **JUANITA** dancing to the music. If room on stage, perhaps music is coming from a jukebox, or it could be from a radio on or behind the bar.)*

G.W.. *(Crying.)* Oh, Peggy, Peggy, Peggy. *(Indicates legs.)* Seventeen years ago these sumbitches killed the love of my life.

ODELL. Well, now technically, it wasn't them sumbitches, G.W. Member? Noleta burnt up them wooden legs that killed Peggy.

G.W.. I know that, you idiot!

ODELL. Well, you don't have to get nasty. Look on the bright side. At least you once had a wife and a mistress. Some of us ain't never found love.

WARDELL. Maybe it's cause no one wants you, Odell.

G.W.. You got that right! Goddamn halfwit.

ODELL. I was struck by lightning! That's why I'm a little slow.

WARDELL. Made you smarter in my opinion!

JUANITA. Princess Margaret was Queen Elizabeth's sister and her former daughter-in-law Sarah Ferguson is a duchess. And Prince Charles had a mistress, Camilla

---

* A license to produce A VERY SORDID WEDDING does not include a performance license for any third-party or copyrighted music. Licensees should create an original composition or use music in the public domain. For further information, please see Music Use Note on page 3.

Parker Bowles. *(Emotional.)* And that's what killed Diana!

WARDELL. Good to know, Juanita.

ODELL. *(To* **WARDELL.***)* Well, I ain't never seen no love in your life neither.

WARDELL. Me and LaVonda had a good thing going at one time.

ODELL. Yeah, 'til she dumped your ass like a million years ago.

> (**ODELL** *completes a string-trick. He proudly shows the simple V to the others.)*

Victory! That's a new one I made up just right now. "V" for victory!

G.W.. *(Evaluates.)* Looks like a big hairless vagina to me.

JUANITA. I don't like that.

WARDELL. I got something that'll make you feel better, G.W.

G.W.. A bullet through my head?

WARDELL. Naw, I'm putting back together that fifteen-year tribute for Peggy that was supposed to have been two years ago. Got derailed by that hail storm and Odell gettin' struck by lightning. And then last year Juanita went missing for two days.

JUANITA. Did you find me?

WARDELL. You got locked in the storage closet, passed out drunk from trying each and every one of my liquors in there.

JUANITA. *(Claps.)* Good times.

ODELL. I never should have tried to catch them hail balls in my mouth like peanuts. Error in judgment.

WARDELL. We'll just make it a seventeen-year anniversary. We can get together and sing Peggy's favorite hymns just like the good ol' days.

G.W.. *(Emotional.)* How's it gonna be like the good ol' days when the love of my life Peggy is six feet under?

JUANITA. *(Leans in, pats his arm, sweetly.)* You can't kill love, G.W. But love can kill you. And you don't want that.

G.W.. Did she just make sense?

WARDELL. Hell, even a blind hog finds an acorn every now and then.

> *(Lights out Bubba's Bar.)*

Scene Six

(Cast: **BROTHER BOY, SISSY, BRENDA** *(Voice over).)*

(Lights up **BROTHER BOY***'s room as he listens to a song in the style of Tammy Wynette's* **["'TIL I CAN MAKE IT ON MY OWN"]**'. **BROTHER BOY** *stirs, gets up, rummages through his gowns, then turns to Tammy's picture, picks it up, looks around.)*

BROTHER BOY.   Come to me, Tammy. I need you. Why don't you ever come to me anymore? *(He waits.)* Well, shit. She ain't a comin'.

*(***BROTHER BOY** *returns the picture to its place, picks up his princess phone, settles on his bed and dials.)*

(Lights up **SISSY***'s house. TV comes to life,* **SISSY** *still fixed on it.)*

BRENDA.   *(On TV.)* No, no, no, no. Not that doll! That doll has special memories!

*(***SISSY***'s phone rings.)*

SISSY.   Aw, bless her heart. *(Mutes TV, answers phone.)* Hello?

---

* A license to produce A VERY SORDID WEDDING does not include a performance license for "'TIL I CAN MAKE IT ON MY OWN". The publisher and author suggest that the licensee contact ASCAP or BMI to ascertain the music publisher and contact such music publisher to license or acquire permission for performance of the song. If a license or permission is unattainable for "'TIL I CAN MAKE IT ON MY OWN", the licensee may not use the song in A VERY SORDID WEDDING but should create an original composition in a similar style or use a similar song in the public domain. For further information, please see Music Use Note on page 3.

BROTHER BOY. Hey, Sissy.

SISSY. Well hello there, Brother Boy! How are you, hon?

BROTHER BOY. Oh, Sissy, I keep having this dream. My fantasies of Wardell and me getting married have started up again. The dream starts so beautiful, the perfect wedding, and you were a bridesmaid!

SISSY. Awww, thanks for asking me.

BROTHER BOY. It was a dream Sissy! But then the dream turns into an awful, awful nightmare, and the wedding becomes Mama's funeral. And when I reach the altar, Mama's coffin is there and Mama bolts up and tells me that she's putting me back into the looney bin with that evil Dr. Eve with them store-bought titties to finish dehomosexualizin' me! Then she starts chasing me with that ratty ol' mink stole.

SISSY. I sold that stole at a yard sale to Saline Hinkle for two dollars.

BROTHER BOY. Well, in my dream, you didn't! Mama was wearing it in her coffin and then she was chasing me with it. I woke up in a cold sweat, Sissy, shiverin' like a Chihuahua!

SISSY. Well, you know that dreams aren't real, sweetie.

BROTHER. *(Testy.)* Yes, I'm well aware of that, Sissy. But you do know what today's date is, don't you?

SISSY. Thursday.

BROTHER BOY. Yes! Mama's death date! She died seventeen years ago. She's haunting me because... Sissy, she never wanted me to be happy!

SISSY. Oh, sweet baby Jesus! How time flies. Seems like just yesterday that Peggy tripped over them wooden legs and hit her head on that nasty ol' sink at the Galaxy Motel while havin' that affair with G.W. Nethercott.

> *(Lights out* **SISSY***'s house and* **BROTHER BOY***'s room.)*

Scene Seven

(Cast: **LATRELLE, TY, KYLE.***)*

(Lights up bench. **LATRELLE**'s *cell phone rings.* **LATRELLE** *digs in her bag for her phone, looks at the screen, then answers it.)*

LATRELLE. Hello, sweet boy!

> *(Lights up on parking lot – on opposite side of stage.* **TY**, *40s,* **LATRELLE**'s *handsome, gay activist son, enters on his cell.)*

TY. Hey Mama! I'm calling you from Dallas!

LATRELLE. Dallas? You're so close. Did you finish your, uh, marriage tour thingamagig?

TY. Yes ma'am. This last part is what I like to call "the weeping and gnashing of teeth" part of the tour. You know, the South, where all the judgmental Christians are weeping and gnashing their teeth because two people who love each other now have equal rights.

LATRELLE. Uh-huh. Well, y'all sure did get a lot of press.

TY. That was the point.

LATRELLE. Yes, great for your cause, not always easy for mothers in Winters, Texas.

TY. Well, I'm sorry that exposing bigotry has caused you such grief, Mama.

LATRELLE. Oh, don't worry about it. I'm used to being gossiped about by now. But, how come you're in Dallas, and I'm just now finding out?

TY. Kyle's up for a big job at Mitchell Gold + Bob Williams. Head design associate, and he gets to choose between Dallas and Atlanta. He's in his final interview right now.

LATRELLE. Oh, choose Dallas! I could come up there and shop. Kyle gets family discounts, right? I need a new chaise, in taupe.

TY. *(Eye roll.)* We'll get right on that.

LATRELLE. And you can visit Winters often.

TY. Yes, that would be… just horrible. Although, maybe we could make Texas number fifty, in Winters, and you could throw us our wedding. That would certainly get lots of attention.

> *(**LATRELLE** gets up, picks up the bouquet she has left at the grave.)*

LATRELLE. Oh, aren't these flowers pretty? It's your Nan Nan's death date. I'm in the cemetery as we speak. I wish you were here, but you'll always find a reason not to visit Winters.

TY. *(Testy.)* I just gave you a reason for me to come home and you changed the subject!

LATRELLE. Oh, let's not fight, Ty. You know I love you, I do, and I'm really happy that you and Kyle have found each other, I just, well, it's just not exactly the kind of wedding that I always envisioned.

TY. Me neither, because I never thought it was possible because I was taught by you, the church and everybody else that –!

> *(**KYLE** enters.)*

*(To **KYLE**.)* My mother.

KYLE. I assumed.

TY. *(Back in phone.)* Okay, you're right, you're right, Mama, let's change the subject. Um, 'cause I've been saving the big news. And I mean big.

> *(**KYLE** grabs the phone from **TY**.)*

KYLE. Hey, Latrelle, what would you prefer to be called? Grandma? Meemaw? Nana? Or my personal favorite because you're so glamorous... Glam-ma.

LATRELLE. Wait. What?! Are y'all?!

KYLE. Yes! Our surrogate just finished her first trimester, and we wanted to wait, you know, just to be sure, but you are going to be a glam-ma! Of twins! And we're moving to Dallas!

TY. We are?

LATRELLE. *(Screams.)* Ahhhh!

KYLE. *(Hands phone back to TY.)* She's screaming.

TY. Scream of happiness or horror?

> (**LATRELLE** *continues screams of happiness as lights out on the bench and parking lot.)*

Scene Eight

(Cast: **LAVONDA, NOLETA, BROTHER BOY, AUNT LITTLE NEECY** *(Off stage).)*

(Lights up on hospital hallway. **NOLETA** *and* **LAVONDA** *enter making their path along the apron of the stage, which serves as the hallway of Winter's Memorial Hospital.* **NOLETA** *is eating a bag of M&M's non-stop.)*

NOLETA. *(Sniffs.)* Hospitals smell so clean!

LAVONDA. Okay, go see your Mama and come get me after. *(Points off stage.)* Aunt Little Neecy is in that room right over there. Just follow the gruntin' sounds.

*(***AUNT LITTLE NEECY** *grunts off stage.)*

NOLETA. Pray for me!

LAVONDA. Honey, you need a lot more than prayers.

*(***LAVONDA***'s cell phone starts ringing.* **NOLETA** *continues on and exits.* **LAVONDA** *pauses to answer the phone, settles up against a wall.)*

(Looks at dial, answers.) Oh, hello there, Brother Boy.

(Lights up **BROTHER BOY***'s room. During the scene, he explores the drag outfits on the rack.)*

BROTHER BOY. LaVonda, I need your help! My talents are being wasted here in Longfuckin'view, Texas. I need you to rescue me.

LAVONDA. Uh-huh. Well, did you hear that the Hitchhiker Murderer has escaped the pen? He's from Longview, you know, and he's killed people all over that area.

Had sex with those he murdered, he's supposed to be executed next week.

BROTHER BOY. LaVonda! Please! You know I frighten easily. I'm as fragile as a little baby kitten, and Mama's ghost is haunting me! And, it's not the good haunting like when Tammy used to come to me, it's the bad haunting. And they've made this new evil drag queen my boss and she has me on probation. She is saying that I have to give up Tammy, I have to give up Loretta, and I have to give up Dolly! I'll have no show! My new show is called "We Three Queens Of Opry Are." I mean who am 'posed to do, LaVonda? Carrie Underwood? Her kind of Christianity frightens me. One minute she's asking for Jesus to take the wheel and then the next minute she's slashin' her cheatin' ex-boyfriend's tires and knockin' out headlights with a baseball bat! Or Blake Shelton's fleshy wife, what's her name?

LAVONDA. Miranda Lambert. They're getting divorced. And she's lost weight.

BROTHER BOY. Well, I hadn't. I'm big as Dallas and half of Fort Worth. I look like my water is about to break. And I can't pull off them young ones, LaVonda. You can just dim the lights just so low and then you're in the dark. I need you to come get me and rescue me from Wrongview, Texas! Borrow Wardell's truck and move me up to Dallas where opportunity is rampant. *(Wistfully.)* I heard about this club called The Rose Room. Seats five hundred people. I need that kind of appreciation, LaVonda. I need that kind of applause. I need that rush. *(Emotional, sinks to bed.)* I need my precious, precious, precious Tammy.

LAVONDA. Now look, I just can't come right now. I'm here at the hospital setting with Evelyn Crawley's Aunt Little Neecy.

BROTHER BOY. Aunt Little Neecy who used to have all them feral cats?

LAVONDA. And a pet skunk!

BROTHER BOY. I thought she died. She was old when we was kids. And why are you setting with the afflicted? LaVonda, that is so unlike you.

LAVONDA. Evelyn has had something on me for years which I do not want to discuss, and she has just been waiting to collect.

BROTHER BOY. What's wrong with Aunt Little Neecy, besides meanness and insanity?

LAVONDA. Well, Evelyn was in her kitchen picklin' okras from her garden, and she put Aunt Little Neecy in front of the television to keep her occupied and to keep her from going through her underwear drawer again. She's just obsessed with Evelyn's underwear, likes to try ever' one of 'em on.

BROTHER BOY. Nothin' crazy about that!

LAVONDA. Well, it, it stretches them out!

BROTHER BOY. Oh.

LAVONDA. Anyway, Aunt Little Neecy just loves that show where the sponges talk, I mean, whoever came up with that show had to be on drugs if you ask me, so Evelyn looks up at the clock on the stove and it's time for...

BROTHER BOY. *(Overlap; covers phone.)* Tammy, honey, is this as boring to you as it is to me?

LAVONDA. ... *The Price Is Right*, although Lord, she was pissed when Bob Barker quit, and hates Drew Carey, who looks better fat. Anyway, she goes in there, tries to change the channel on the TV, and that's when the trouble started.

BROTHER BOY. That is a lotta detail, LaVonda.

LAVONDA. Oh hush, you asked! And I listen to your sob sister stories every fuckin' day!

BROTHER BOY. Okay, okay. Proceed.

LAVONDA. Well, it became a battle over that remote. Evelyn could not pry that remote out of Aunt Little Neecy's hand, grip of death, and during the struggle, that remote landed up 'side Evelyn's head. Well, that did it! Evelyn lost her temper, Aunt Little Neecy lost hers! So, right in the middle of Aunt Little Neecy's big ol' temper tantrum, she goes into a full-blown epileptic seizure and bit off her tongue.

BROTHER BOY. Bit off her tongue?!

LAVONDA. Yes!

BROTHER BOY. Lord!

LAVONDA. Evelyn had to put that bit-off tongue in the pickle jar she was using for putting up her okra, dumped that good okra right in the sink, packed that jar with ice.

BROTHER BOY. Quick thinkin'!

LAVONDA. Sure was. And she got Aunt Little Neecy here to the hospital where Dr. Lloyd was able to reattach that bit-off tongue. But all that blood just ruined Evelyn's brand new white carpet. Indoor, outdoor. Evelyn says that the good news is that the doctors say that Aunt Little Neecy will speak again with speech therapy, which in my humble opinion is not good news 'cause that crazy old bat never fuckin' shuts up! And I strongly believe that Evelyn will regret packing that tongue on ice!

BROTHER BOY. What does Evelyn have on you anyway?!

LAVONDA. Well, it has to do with her witnessing a justified crime that I was an accomplice to years ago, involving a goat.

BROTHER BOY. Oh my god, was it sexual?

LAVONDA. No! And that is all you need to know.

BROTHER BOY. Well, Evelyn was just plain stupid buying that white carpet. But, LaVonda, honey, I'm desperate. I need for you to come up here and take me to Dallas!

AUNT LITTLE NEECY. *(Off stage.)* Uhhhhhgghh!!!!!

(A TV remote comes flying past **LAVONDA***'s head.)*

LAVONDA. Uh-oh. That crazy ol' bitch is throwing things, I gotta go.

(Lights out on hospital hallway as **LAVONDA** *picks up the remote and exits. Lights out on* **BROTHER BOY***'s room as he hangs up in defeat.)*

Scene Nine

(Cast: **JIMMY RAY, MRS. BARNES, LATRELLE***).)*

(Lights up bench. **LATRELLE** *rises, walks over to Mama's grave.)*

LATRELLE. Well, Mama, the news just keeps rolling in. You're going to be a great-grandmother and I'm going to be a Glam-ma...of twins! I'm just going to skip all the conception details because even beyond the grave, I'm not sure you can handle them. *(Gets emotional.)* There's not a day that goes by that I don't miss you, Mama – and I wish... I just wish that that ingrate G.W. Nethercott had never taken off those legs that fateful night...or that you had just turned on a light when you went to the bathroom in that nasty motel room. But... as they say, hindsight is twenty-twenty. And here we are.

> *(Lights up on church sign.* **JIMMY RAY BREWTON** *and* **MRS. BARNES,** *the older church secretary, once the pastor's wife, work on the new signage. When finished the sign will read: ANTI-EQUALITY REVIVAL – STARTS THIS FRIDAY!)*

JIMMY RAY. Just need an "A" and a "Y".

> *(***LATRELLE** *spots the duo creating the signage.)*

LATRELLE. Bye, bye, Mama.

> *(***MRS. BARNES** *digs and produces the letters.)*

MRS. BARNES. Here's a "Y". *(Hands it to* **JIMMY RAY.***)* And an "A".

> *(***LATRELLE** *fixes on the sign for a moment, then walks over. Lights out on bench.)*

LATRELLE. Woo hoo, Mrs. Barnes!

MRS. BARNES. Oh, oh, hello, Latrelle. You've gotta meet the new preacher. Jimmy Ray. Reverend Jimmy Ray Brewton. He's my nephew and he's gonna carry on now that Cecil has gone on to glory to meet Jesus. Jimmy Ray, this is Latrelle Williamson. She's the one I told you about... *(Whispers.)* ...with the son.

*(**LATRELLE** shoots **MRS. BARNES** a look.)*

JIMMY RAY. Well, the good Lord sure did bless you with beauty, Latrelle.

LATRELLE. *(Flattered.)* Oh...well –

JIMMY RAY. He did indeed.

LATRELLE. Well, thank you. I have a question. Now that marriage equality is the law of the land... *(Points to sign.)* How is this revival, well, gonna change things?

JIMMY RAY. The Supreme Court's not the law of this land. The word of God is the law of this land.

LATRELLE. Well, actually, if memory serves me right, that's not exactly true. The Constitution is the law of the land, not the Bible. Separation of church and state. Something we all should have been taught in school.

JIMMY RAY. She's a feisty one, ain't she?

MRS. BARNES. Indeed she is. Oh, I could tell you stories.

LATRELLE. I'm sure you already have.

JIMMY RAY. The fact of the matter is five liberal justices and an ungodly Muslim president can't take away my... your... biblical and constitutional right to live according to your deeply held beliefs.

LATRELLE. Well, now you've lost me. Because, as I said, it's the law.

JIMMY RAY. Well, that's true, but as Christian warriors, we have to fight for our Lord. And here's your answer. We are gonna make Runnels County a sanctuary county for the institution of biblical marriage, one man, one woman, and to never have a gay marriage performed in this county.

MRS. BARNES. Ever ever ever! We want our rainbow back!

JIMMY RAY. We do indeed. There have been consequences to the moral decay of this country caused by the gays and the acceptance of their lifestyle and there will be more. Nine-eleven, AIDS, Obama's election, Hurricane Katrina.

MRS. BARNES. And Sandy. And don't forget that Japanese tsunami. And fire ants! All because of the gays.

LATRELLE. You know, I consider myself a God-fearing Christian, but I find it hard to believe that the gays wield enough power to control the weather... and disease... and insects.

JIMMY RAY. Allow me to correct you here. You see, God has the power to respond appropriately to immorality, and it's our responsibility to protect this county from his wrath.

MRS. BARNES. Amen.

LATRELLE. Well, things become a little cloudy and complicated when... *(Pointedly to* MRS. BARNES.*)* I'm sure you've been told that my son is gay.

JIMMY RAY. Yes, I have heard that, and I am so, so sorry. That cross must be so hard for you to carry. Now, you just might need this revival more than anybody in this town. Won't you come by on Friday, Latrelle? And I promise you that everything will become crystal clear.

LATRELLE. Hmm. You know what, I think I will.

JIMMY RAY & MRS. BARNES. Amen! Praise the Lord!

(Lights out on church sign.)

Scene Ten

(Cast: **HORTENSE, NOLETA.***)*

(Lights up on hospital room #1. **HORTENSE,**
NOLETA*'s mean, ancient mother, lies in the
bed, wearing a bright muumuu. A vase
of flowers with a string of "get well soon"
balloons attached sits on the bedside table.
Note: This bed should be one where the
occupant can sit up, hospital style.* **NOLETA**
*enters, eating her M&Ms throughout the
scene.)*

HORTENSE. What took you so long?! Did you bring me my
PayDay and my flamingo pink lipstick?! The nurses,
the orderlies, the new preacher had to look at me all
day without my lips on!

NOLETA. Yes, ma'am. I'm sorry.

HORTENSE. Oh, just give me my lipstick! If I'm going to
die, I want to look presentable. *(Picks up hand mirror,
looks.)* Oh, just cremate me. You would never be able to
do these eyebrows.

NOLETA. Mama, you are not going to die!

HORTENSE. Stomach cancer runs in this family! You're
probably going to die of it too. *(Yells.)* Just give me my
lipstick and my PayDay!

NOLETA. *(Digs in her purse.)* Okay. Oh, there it is!

*(She pulls out the missing ponytail, tosses
it on* **HORTENSE***'s bed, who slaps it with her
church fan.)*

HORTENSE. Oh, kill it!

*(***NOLETA** *pulls out a PayDay, hands it to*
HORTENSE.*)*

NOLELA. PayDay.

HORTENSE. PayDay, good.

> (**NOLETA** *pulls out a tube of lipstick and hands it to* **HORTENSE.**)

NOLETA. Lipstick.

HORTENSE. Lipstick. And quit eating! You'll never get another man at your size!

NOLETA. Mama, I'm a size ten!

> (*Note: Size can be adjusted according to the actress cast.* **NOLETA** *should lie by one size down to make the joke work.*)

HORTENSE. In what country?

NOLETA. I am not gonna let you push my buttons, Mama. You may have installed 'em, but I am not going to let you push them. I heard that on Oprah's Life Classes.

HORTENSE. Oh shut up! Oprah's full of shit!

NOLETA. (*Gasps, clutches her chest.*) Now, if you'll excuse me, I am going to see if they have your pending tests back to see how much longer I have to put up with this shit – which Oprah is NOT full of!

> (**NOLETA** *storms out, putting on the ponytail. Lights out hosptial room #1.*)

> (*Lights up hospital hallway.* **NOLETA** *crosses the apron of the stage.*)

(*Quietly.*) LaVonda! (*Then yelling.*) LaVonda!

> (**NURSE SAMPLE,** *a nurse with a permanent scowl, enters the opposite side of the hallway, passing* **NOLETA.**)

NURSE SAMPLE. No yelling in the hallways! There are sick people in here. Didn't your mother teach you to be considerate?

NOLETA. No ma'am. She just taught me to feel inferior and worthless.

NURSE SAMPLE. Trash.

> (**NOLETA** *continues on, exits. Lights out hospital hallway.*)

Scene Eleven

(Cast: **SISSY, VERA, LATRELLE.***)*

(Lights up **SISSY**'s *house.* **SISSY** *is reading her Bible.)*

SISSY. "Come, Lord Jesus! The grace of the Lord Jesus be with all. Amen." Hmm. That's not the best endin' if you ask me.

> (**SISSY** *puts her Bible down on the coffee table as a car drives up.)*

LATRELLE. *(Off stage.)* Sissy! Sissy!

SISSY. *(Mutters.)* Oh Lord, that's Latrelle.

> (**SISSY** *gets up, grabs her Valium bottle, dry swallows a couple.* **LATRELLE** *storms in.)*

LATRELLE. Sissy! Well, you're just never gonna believe what the church is doing, you just won't. They're having an Anti-Equality Revival! That's what they're calling it. Starts tomorrow. I just met the new preacher. Jimmy Ray Brewton. So handsome, but very argumentative.

SISSY. Well, you'd know all about that.

LATRELLE. That's not always a bad thing. Oh! And I just hung up from Ty. He and Kyle are moving to Dallas. Kyle's got a big job offer from a very upscale, high end, designer furniture store! *(Looks around in judgment.)* Maybe you can get some free furniture. Oh! But the bigger news is… the boys are having twins! Their surrogate just got past her first trimester!

SISSY. Awwww, twins!

LATRELLE. I'm going to be a grandmother, Sissy! Kyle came up with the cutest name for me… Glam-ma… since he thinks I'm glamorous.

SISSY. Glam-ma. Awwww. That's cute. Help me understand how this works, Latrelle, how the boys are having twins with this –?

LATRELLE. Surrogate. Well, it's very complicated. Very scientific, very legal. But basically, both boys contributed... *(Whispers)* ...sperm, so each will have their own biological child.

> *(SISSY grabs her tumbler from the coffee table and trots off to the kitchen.)*

SISSY. *(Exiting.)* Uh-huh.

> *(LATRELLE opens her purse, grabs a compact, powders down and reapplies her makeup as she yells to SISSY.)*

LATRELLE. Then they purchased eggs from an egg donor that they choose from some pictures and biographies of potential donors on a top-secret internet site. Then they hired a separate surrogate who is now carrying the babies. There's this place called Growing Generations that puts the whole thing together.

> *(SISSY returns with two tumblers, hands one to LATRELLE, then sits by her on the sofa.)*

SISSY. Lord, that's complicated. How much does all this run?

LATRELLE. One hundred and fifty thousand. Package deal!

SISSY. Sweet baby Jesus, that's high! So... to make these babies... Ty and Kyle did what Peggy used to say killed baby kittens? The very thing that young boys do into socks that they throw under the bed –

LATRELLE. How do you know that?

SISSY. Ty used to spend summers with me! I thought he was losing socks, then mystery was solved when I found a bunch under the bed! So they both do their business in a cup instead of a sock, then it goes to some science lab, where it then fertilizes some stray woman's eggs that they choose from that top secret internet site. Then the fertilized eggs are put into the surrogate's uterus that will then carry the babies.

LATRELLE. Yes!

SISSY. And that oldest Winkler girl just had her fourth baby out of wedlock. They coulda just slipped her a twenty and had a little white trash baby!

LATRELLE. No, thank you. I do not want a Winkler grandchild. No tellin' what's swimming in that gene pool. Besides, they wanted their own. And with today's technology, each one can have their very own biological child.

SISSY. Awww. One white one and one cute little mulatto. Oooh, I hope the mulatto one is a girl. Halle Berry is so beautiful.

LATRELLE. Sissy, that word, mulatto, is no longer politically correct. Mixed is preferred.

SISSY. Mixed, huh? Well, if you say so. Mulatto sure has a prettier ring to it. Lord, I cannot keep up.

> (**SISSY** *gets up and gets a writing pad and pen from her drawer, opens it and starts scratching out and writing.*)

Is African-American still right?

LATRELLE. I believe so, only there are some who don't care for that either. Oh, I cannot wait to tell mid-life crisis Wilson that he's gonna be a grandpa! I gotta go tittle.

> (**LATRELLE** *exits, squirming.* **SISSY** *looks around.*)

SISSY. What's wrong with my furniture?

(**SISSY** *thinks a moment, then picks up her phone, dials while lighting a cigarette.*)

(*Lights up The Corner Stop.* **VERA LISSO**, *the large, bigoted* **CASHIER**, *sits on her stool behind the counter that houses a cash register, a phone, maybe a chip stand, some cigarettes behind her. During scene* **VERA** *pulls pieces from a pink Hostess SnoBall and wraps cheese balls in it. She eats her snack as she answers the phone.*)

VERA. Corner Stop, where Jesus is alive and well and everything is convenient. This is Vera, how may I help you?

SISSY. Hello, Vera. Well, I just now finished reading the entire Bible. Latrelle just stopped by and I've been dealin' with Brother Boy this morning. More troubles than Christ on the cross.

VERA. Well, bless his heart. I've been praying for Jesus to turn him straight.

SISSY. Well, Vera, I think perhaps that is a wasted prayer.

VERA. "If you have faith the size of a mustard seed, you can say to a mulberry tree, 'be uprooted and be planted in the sea.'" That's in Luke. (*Yells off stage.*) Leticia, you're mixing up the Sweet Spicy Chili Doritos with the Spicy Nachos again!

SISSY. "Be ye kind, one to another," Ephesians 4:32.

VERA. Uh-huh. That's one of my favorites.

SISSY. Why do you think anybody would want to uproot a mulberry tree and plant it in the sea? How would they pick their mulberries? There are some things in the Bible that just do not make a lick of sense to me.

VERA. Well, I live by the Bible, Sissy, I don't need it to make sense. Now, I'm gonna need you on my Anti-Equality

Callin' Committee. The revival starts tomorrow, and we gotta get the final word out. They're coming for our religious freedom and good Christians are being persecuted.

SISSY. By who?

VERA. Obama, Hillary Clinton, five liberal judges and Miley Cyrus. *(Spots Leticia off stage, screams.)* Leticia, that's not right! *(In phone.)* Sissy I have to go. *(Hangs up, yelling.)* Do I have to climb down off this stool and do everything myself!??

> *(Lights fade corner stop as* VERA *struggles to get off of her stool.)*

SISSY. *(Quietly.)* Be ye kind, one to another.

> *(Lights out* SISSY's *house as she hangs up the phone.)*

Scene Twelve

(Cast: **NOLETA, HARDY.***)*

(Lights up hospital hallway as **NOLETA** *crosses back, still looking for* **LAVONDA.***)*

NOLETA. LaVonda! *(Louder.)* LaVonda!

(Lights up on hospital room #2, just slight redress of #1. As **NOLETA** *passes it,* **HARDY** *takes note.)*

HARDY. Hey pretty lady, could you come in here?

NOLETA. Me?

HARDY. Well, I don't see no other pretty lady nearby.

(Lights out on hospital hallway as **NOLETA** *tentatively enters the room, mesmerized by this gorgeous man.)*

Hey, would you be an angel and hand me them crutches over there? That goddamn mean nurse helped me to this chair and told me she'd be back in thirty minutes, been over an hour. Damnation, you're perty. And I don't see no wedding ring.

NOLETA. *(Holds up her finger.)* No, no more, no ring. I pawned it after my divorce seventeen years ago. Single. See, my husband had an affair on me with my best friend's seventy-year-old mother and our friendship survived but the marriage did not. My friend, LaVonda, that's Peggy's daughter... Peggy is the old, adulterating dead woman, is setting in that room across from you with Evelyn Crawley's Aunt Little Neecy. Aunt Little Neecy is crazy as a sack full of assholes. Bless her heart. And I'm here visiting my mama who either has stomach cancer or a severe case of ptomaine. I mean, we're prayin' that it's ptomaine, but she is so damn mean, sometimes I just wish she would die. Oh shoot, I meant to just think that. My husband G.W., well, my ex-husband now, seventeen years, no ring, single. He is a Vietnam vet and he has two wooden legs, well technically they're fiberglass, and one day I got real mad and I took one of them legs and I bashed in all the windows on his pickup truck while he was takin' a bath. Not a pretty sight with them stubs. Years ago. Then, I set them legs on fire in the bed of his pickup truck bein's as I was so upset after Peggy's funeral, ya know, about the affair, not her death. But first, I soaked them legs in gasoline, 'cause I think that shit through. Tossed in a match... Boom! It's hard to make a marriage work after that.

HARDY. Remind me to never piss you off.

NOLETA. *(Giggles.)* Okay.

HARDY. I, uh, I don't mean to make ya nervous.

NOLETA. *(Giggles.)* What happened to your leg?

HARDY. I crushed it working on an oil rig. *(Points.)* Uh, my crutches.

NOLETA. Oh, right. Sorry.

> *(She rushes over, grabs his crutches, hands them to him.)*

Okay, here ya go.

HARDY. Thank you. Hey, will you get behind me, put both your hands around my waist and give me a shove up?

NOLETA. Okay.

HARDY. Don't look at my ass.

NOLETA. Okay.

> *(**NOLETA** places her hands around **HARDY**'s waist, gives him the shove-up he requested.*

As he rises, his exposed ass shines out of the
hospital gown mooning the audience.)

Oh yay! It worked!

(She immediately is transfixed on his ass.)

HARDY. My buddy Hank's supposed to bring me some
sweats, but... are you looking at my ass?

NOLETA. No. Well, maybe just a little.

(He turns, drops the crutches, falls on the
bed.)

HARDY. Good.

*(**NOLETA** falls on top of him.)*

NOLETA. Oh, Lord!

(They aggressively begin to kiss. As clothes
fly, lights out on hospital room #2.)

Scene Thirteen

(Cast: **VERA, SISSY, LATRELLE.***)*

(Lights up on The Corner Stop. **VERA** *is ringing up many cartons of cigarettes for* **SISSY. SISSY** *puts them in her shopping bag as* **VERA** *hands them to her, one by one.)*

VERA. $52.09, $52.09, $52.09, $52.09, $52.09, $52.09, $52.09, $52.09 and $52.09. Will there be anything else?

SISSY. Uh-uh, no ma'am, no, no, no. For that, I can't even afford to eat anymore!

VERA. Have you given any more thought to being on my Anti-Equality Callin' Committee?

SISSY. Well, I –

*(***LATRELLE*** enters, rushing up to the counter with a Baby Ruth candy bar.)*

LATRELLE. Sissy, will you buy me this Baby Ruth? I had a cravin' for something sweet.

VERA. *(Fake sweet.)* Well, hello Latrelle. I heard that your ex-husband has been shackin' up with a much, much younger, more beautiful woman in your former mini-mansion that you lost in the divorce over in San Angelo. How you holding up, hon?

LATRELLE. I'm fine, Vera. Thank you.

VERA. Well, you've been on my prayer list ever since your husband ran off with that mulatto, IHOP waitress.

SISSY. Prayers mean so much. "Mulatto" is no longer politically correct, Vera. They prefer "mixed" these days.

LATRELLE. And I've been praying for you and your struggle with obesity and gluttony, too. "If you have faith, you can move a mountain."

VERA. I am not a glutton! I have glandular problems!

SISSY. Latrelle, Vera has struggled so with her weight battle. Ever since we were kids. Dr. Oz says it's a disease, just like being a alcoholic.

LATRELLE. Well, then perhaps it's time for you to get sober.

VERA. *(Leaning in.)* People don't like you, Latrelle.

LATRELLE. *(Also leaning in.)* Yes, it's the one thing we have in common, Vera. C'mon Sissy.

>*(They start out, then* **LATRELLE** *turns back and angrily smashes* **VERA***'s stash of food that sits on the counter. Lights out on The Corner Stop as* **VERA** *reacts.)*

Scene Fourteen

(Cast: **NOLETA, HARDY, LAVONDA.***)*

(Lights up on hospital room #2. **NOLETA** *and* **HARDY** *sit up in the bed, post coitus, smoking.* **HARDY** *is shirtless.)*

(Lights up hospital hallway as **LAVONDA** *enters and passes* **HARDY***'s room.)*

NOLETA. *(Spots* **LAVONDA***.)* LaVonda. LaVonda!

*(***LAVONDA** *enters the room, mouth agape.)*

This is Hardy. Hardy, this is LaVonda. Hardy's new in town.

LAVONDA. And who are you? The Welcome Wagon? Are you two smoking in the hospital?

HARDY. Oh, yeah, we were smokin' alright!

NOLETA. *(To* **HARDY***.)* I gotta go, I'm late for work.

*(***NOLETA** *gets up, buttons her blouse and* **HARDY** *slaps her on the ass.)*

HARDY. We're not done here, okay?

NOLETA. *(Giggling like a school girl.)* Okay!

*(***NOLETA** *takes a pen out of her purse and writes on* **HARDY***'s cast.)*

That's my cell phone number. I don't answer blocked calls 'cause of bill collectors.

(Lights out on hospital room #2 as **LAVONDA** *and* **NOLETA** *exit into hospital hallway.)*

LAVONDA. Why don't anything good like this ever happen in my life?

NOLETA. Did you see the size of his feet?

LAVONDA. I sure did. Come on! We gotta get you to work.

> *(As* **LAVONDA** *and* **NOLETA** *exit, lights out hospital hallway.)*

Scene Fifteen

(Cast: **BROTHER BOY, BILLY JOE, MARTY.***)*

(Lights up on Sidetracks, a sad little gay bar in Longview, Texas. On one wall or door, a "We Three Queens Of Opry Are" poster is featured and three wig heads have been placed on a small table by the stage. Perhaps a gay flag has been hung somewhere and some other gay décor. On the tiny stage, **BROTHER BOY** *rummages through his rack of costumes, humming a song in the style of Tammy Wynette's* **["WOMANHOOD"]** *for his show. He evaluates one gown.)*

BROTHER BOY. Velcro, girl, Velcro! That'll solve this shit.

(He hears a door open. **BILLY JOE DOBSON***, the hot, dark brooding serial killer enters.)*

Hello? We're not open yet.

BILLY JOE. Hello.

*(***BROTHER BOY** *turns to see* **BILLY JOE** *swaggering towards him.)*

You okay?

*(***BROTHER BOY** *scrambles to put on the Tammy wig.)*

---

* A license to produce A VERY SORDID WEDDING does not include a performance license for "WOMANHOOD". The publisher and author suggest that the licensee contact ASCAP or BMI to ascertain the music publisher and contact such music publisher to license or acquire permission for performance of the song. If a license or permission is unattainable for "WOMANHOOD", the licensee may not use the song in A VERY SORDID WEDDING but should create an original composition in a similar style or use a similar song in the public domain. For further information, please see Music Use Note on page 3.

BROTHER BOY. Ah! Forgive my appearance. I'm working on the transition from Tammy into Loretta. It's part of a little skit I come up with for the big show. It's Loretta... my precious Tammy then Dolly. "We Three Queens of Opry Are".

BILLY JOE. *(Charming smile.)* How 'bout you be a good little girl and pour me a strong drink.

BROTHER BOY. We ain't open yet. *(Then quickly.)* Okay.

> *(**BROTHER BOY** heads to the bar.)*

What's your pleasure?

BILLY JOE. Bourbon over ice if it's not too much trouble.

BROTHER BOY. *(Flirting.)* No trouble at all, but I can tell you are.

> *(**BROTHER BOY** stumbles in his heels. **BILLY JOE** grabs his arm.)*

BILLY JOE. *(Charming.)* Here, let me help you.

BROTHER BOY. Well, my, my, my, my. A gentleman caller.

BILLY JOE. Baby, I am no gentleman.

> *(**BROTHER BOY** lands behind the bar and starts fixing a couple of drinks.)*

BROTHER BOY. I'm Earl. But most folks just call me Brother Boy. Or Tammy Wynette.

BILLY JOE. I'm Billy Joe.

> *(**BILLY JOE** just smiles a killer's smile, then spots **BROTHER BOY**'s woman's cigarette case and lighter sitting on the bar.)*

Can I bum a smoke?

BROTHER BOY. Why don't you light two at once. Sorry, they're a little girly.

> (**BILLY JOE** *lights two at once, hands one to* **BROTHER BOY**.)

BILLY JOE. (*Blowing the smoke.*) I'm bisexual. I'll channel my feminine side.

BROTHER BOY. (*Smitten, smoking.*) Bisexual, huh? I know what that tear-drop tattoo means. It means you've been in the pokey.

> (**BROTHER BOY** *slides the drink over.*)

There ya go.

> (*They toast, then* **BILLY JOE** *downs the drink in one gulp.*)

BILLY JOE. Damn, I needed that. I've had a real bad day. You know who I am?

> (**BROTHER BOY** *pours him another drink.*)

BROTHER BOY.   Uh-un. Should I? You famous? My precious, precious Tammy was famous. It was her blessing and her curse. (*Whispers.*) Pills.

BILLY JOE. I'm just a lost soul roaming the highways.

BROTHER BOY. Well, that's poetic. You know, I like the way you look. Rough.

BILLY JOE. Rough trade.

BROTHER BOY. Rough trade.

BILLY JOE. Yeah, I'm rough alright. You know why they call it the pokey?

> (**BILLY JOE** *does the "fucking sign" with index finger on one hand going in and out of a hole he's formed with index finger and thumb on other hand.*)

BROTHER BOY. Oh, that's nasty!

BILLY JOE. Yeah, but you might like to get poked in the pokey.

BROTHER BOY. Oh, you shut up!

BILLY JOE. Be right back. Forgot something in my truck.

> (**BROTHER BOY** *watches* **BILLY JOE** *exit, smitten.*)

BROTHER BOY. Be still my foolish heart.

> (**BROTHER BOY** *returns to his rehearsal, starts organizing the wigs and gowns.* **MARTY WELLS**, *an effeminate man perhaps in full or partial drag, with over-plucked eyebrows, sashays in, slams door.*)

Hello? Billy Joe?

> (**MARTY** *sees the outfits.*)

MARTY. What the hell is all this?

BROTHER BOY. *(Turning.)* Well, hello, Marty. It's nice to be greeted by such a ray of sunshine.

MARTY. Shut up! Who the hell is Billy Joe?

BROTHER BOY. Um... My imaginary friend who watches me rehearse. Billy Joe McAllister. Contrary to popular belief, he did not jump off the Tallahatchie Bridge.

MARTY. You are certifiable! When the hell are you going learn, huh? This is not working, okay?

BROTHER BOY. Oh-kkaaay.

MARTY. And if you can't perform some new material and not the tired old shit from the has-been dead and the has-been almost-dead, then you leave me no choice but to fire your prissy, untalented ass.

BROTHER BOY. Loretta and Dolly are not almost dead! And they are certainly not has-beens! They are country legends! And yes, Loretta's had some health issues, but that was because her favorite son Jack Benny Lynn drowned in that tragic horse accident and she started pillin' again and took to her bed! Who wouldn't? Then she lost the love of her life, Doolittle – and most recently her daughter Betty Lynn. Triple whammy! But she's better now and Dolly is in perfect health and is still performing worldwide and is running Dollywood! Tammy's the only one dead and she is not and will never be a has-been. She's just… gone! And I promised her to carry on her legacy, so she will never be forgotten. I was chosen, Marty. I don't even think you are capable of understanding that kind of commitment and obligation. Tammy's ghost come to me over and over again at the loony bin in Big Springs and –

MARTY.   Shut. The. Fuck. UP! I cannot hear that cockamamie, bullshit country legend ghost story again. You were in a mental institution for a reason, okay? Case closed!

> (**MARTY** *rushes over and rips down the "We Three Queens" poster, tears it up.*)

BROTHER BOY.   Uh-un! Uh-un! Martina! Don't! Ah! No, no! Please don't make me do Carrie Underwood! Or Blake Shelton's formerly fleshy ex-wife or that butch one from Sugarland. I can't do it Marty. I just can't! So why don't you just make like a tree and leave!

MARTY.   I'm not going anywhere! I'm your new boss. The one who had no say in hiring you but can sure as shit fire you. So, come up with a new act or you can hang up your tired, tattered heels!

> (**BILLY JOE** *walks back in, holding a sledge hammer behind his back.*)

BILLY JOE.   Apologize to the lady.

MARTY. Who are you... and what... what are you doing in here?

BILLY JOE. Fuck you!

MARTY. Excuse me?! Just who the hell do you think you're talking to?

BILLY JOE. I'm talking to you, bitch! Now apologize to the lady or you have me to fuckin' deal with.

MARTY. You have about ten seconds to leave this bar before I call the police to have your dumb, redneck, white trash ass arrested.

BILLY JOE. Alright then.

> (**BILLY JOE** *suddenly lunges for* **MARTY,** *sledge hammer drawn, ready to strike.* **BROTHER BOY** *screams like a woman, as does* **MARTY.**)

MARTY & BROTHER BOY. AH! OH!

> (**BROTHER BOY** *grabs for the sledge hammer and starts slapping* **BILLY JOE** *on the arm, over and over.*)

BROTHER BOY. *(Overlap.)* You can't kill him!

MARTY. Oh my god, that's the escaped hitchhiker murderer!

> (**MARTY** *dives behind the bar, grabs a pistol, fires a shot.* **BILLY JOE** *dodges the bullet. Dolly's wighead is hit and falls.*)

BROTHER BOY. No, no, don't shoot him! Don't shoot him! You can't shoot him in the head!

BILLY JOE. You just shot at the wrong person, asswipe!

> (**BILLY JOE** *rushes* **MARTY** *and grabs for the gun, which falls out of* **MARTY's** *trembling hands and hits the floor.* **BROTHER BOY** *grabs*

> *the gun and points it at* **BILLY JOE**, *trembling.*
> **MARTY** *continues to overlap screams,*
> *petrified.)*

BROTHER BOY. I got it, I got it, I got the gun!

MARTY. AH!

BROTHER BOY. No, no, no, no, no!

MARTY. AHHHHH!

> (**BILLY JOE** *grabs his sledge hammer to swing*
> *at* **MARTY** *again.)*

BROTHER BOY. Don't! You'll splatter blood on my costumes
and I've worked so hard on 'em.

BILLY JOE. You gotta be shittin' me.

BROTHER BOY. No, I am not shitting you. Blood and
splattered brains is so messy. Blood will not come out
of chiffon!

MARTY. She's right about that!

BROTHER BOY. No! I mean it Billy Joe, don't you kill him!

> (**BILLY JOE** *assesses the situation, then nods,*
> *goes over and takes the gun from* **BROTHER**
> **BOY** *and points it right in* **MARTY**'s *face.)*

BILLY JOE. Alright then. *(To* **MARTY**.*)* This never happened.
'Cause if one call is made to the cops... *(Traces gun from*
MARTY's *groin to his face.)* ... I will come back here and
slice you from your asshole to your appetite. Got it?

MARTY. I do. This never happened!

> (**BILLY JOE** *turns and starts out,* **BROTHER**
> **BOY** *just staring after him.)*

BILLY JOE. *(Turns back to* **BROTHER BOY**.*)* You comin' or
not?

BROTHER BOY. Well, I guess so. Under the circumstances, my options are rather limited. *(Points to trembling* **MARTY.***)* Watch her. I need to get my shit! *(In* **MARTY***'s face.)* Bye Martina, you fuckin' asshole! I quit!

> *(***BROTHER BOY*** *starts gathering up his belongings as* **BILLY JOE** *continues to point the gun at a trembling* **MARTY***. Lights out on Sidetracks.)*

Scene Sixteen

(Cast: **WARDELL, ODELL, G.W., JUANITA, LAVONDA, NOLETA.***)*

(Lights up on exterior of Bubba's Bar. **WARDELL** *and* **ODELL** *are hanging a banner;* **JUANITA** *and* **G.W.** *hovering nearby, watching. The banner reads:)*

PEGGY INGRAM'S MEMORIAL SINGSPIRATION FRIDAY NIGHT 7PM

G.W.. A little to the right, Wardell.

JUANITA. *(To* **G.W.***)* And those beautiful princes, William and Harry, were left motherless, and I will never forgive Camilla Parker Bowles!

G.W.. Oh, who gives a shit, Juanita?

JUANITA. *(Thinks.)* Queen Elizabeth!

> *(Lights up street.* **LAVONDA** *and* **NOLETA** *enter, walking across the apron, towards the bar folks.)*

LAVONDA. *(Touched.)* Oh, look! They are honoring my Mama! I need to stop for a minute and say hello. *(Calling.)* Hey, Wardell.

NOLETA. Well, hurry. I'm late for work! Roger's gonna kill me.

WARDELL. Hey, Vonie.

> *(***G.W.** *turns and spots* **NOLETA.***)*

LAVONDA. *(To* **NOLETA.***)* There's G.W. Now behave yourself.

> *(***NOLETA** *hangs back.* **LAVONDA** *continues on as* **JUANITA** *staggers towards her.)*

JUANITA. *(To* LAVONDA.*)* And Diana will never see those grand babies of Prince William and Kate Middleton, the Duke and Duchess of Cambridge.

LAVONDA. Tragic, Juanita.

>   *(*JUANITA *exits.* G.W. *spots* NOLETA *and starts tentatively walking towards her.)*

Hey G.W., Odell. Wardell, are y'all doing all this for my Mama?

>   *(*NOLETA *glares at* G.W., *as he makes his way towards her, then she pulls out an emery board and starts filing her nails.)*

WARDELL. Yep, and I'd like you to come tomorrow, as my date. For old time's sake.

LAVONDA. Your date, huh? Well... I think I'd like that.

WARDELL. Me too.

>   *(*WARDELL *puts his arm around* LAVONDA *as they admire the sign.* G.W. *reaches* NOLETA. *He smiles like an idiot.)*

NOLETA. What?

G.W.. Just wanted to pass the howdy. What's up?

NOLETA. Well, Mama's in the hospital. Either stomach cancer or ptomaine, and she told me I'd never get another man at my size. Then right after she said that, I got laid by a younger man, hot as hell, with both legs and <u>very</u> big feet. In a hospital bed. Mama was wrong! So, what's up with you, G.W.? Stayin' busy?

>   *(*G.W., *defeated, returns to the others.)*

LAVONDA. See y'all tomorrow. Bye Wardell. C'mon, Noleta.

>   *(They exit.)*

WARDELL. Bye, Vonie. Can't wait.

(Lights out on exterior of Bubba's Bar and street.)

Scene Seventeen

*(Cast: **ROGER, SISSY, LATRELLE, LAVONDA, NOLETA, VERA, MRS. BARNES.**)*

*(Lights up on The Beehive. Simple. Maybe one beauty salon chair is rolled out and a couple of chairs for waiting customers. **ROGER** stands in the doorway, looking at his watch, irritated.)*

ROGER. *(Mutters.)* Late again.

> *(**SISSY** and **LATRELLE** rush in. **LATRELLE** is carrying a hanging bag, places it over a chair.)*

SISSY. Roger. Hey, hon.

> *(They exchange hugs.)*

ROGER. Why, hello, Sissy. Lord, Latrelle, your hair means harm.

LATRELLE. I know. I missed my standin' last week. Do you think you can fit me in? I want to look twenty-five again!

> *(**ROGER** lifts up his rattail comb as **LATRELLE** sits in the beauty salon chair, **SISSY** sits in another chair, pulls out her "politically correct" notepad and starts studying it.)*

ROGER. Darlin', this is a rattail comb, not a magic wand.

LATRELLE. Now don't make me beat you with that comb! *(Laughs at her joke.)* Wilson, you know, my ex-husband, who I like to refer to as "The Asshole" –

SISSY. *(Overlap.)* Latrelle!

LATRELLE. ...is now living with a so-called singer who performs in the bar inside The San Angelo Bowl-A-Rama. Trash. No class. I'm planning a little surprise visit and want him to be filled with regret the moment he sees me.

ROGER. Well, revenge is a dish best served looking fantastic. Let's get started on this rat's nest.

   (**ROGER** *gets to work on* **LATRELLE***'s hair.*)

SISSY. *(Mutters.)* African-American, Asian, mixed.

   (**NOLETA** *rushes in, followed by* **LAVONDA**, *who stands by the door, lights a cigarette.*)

NOLETA. Roger, I am so, so sorry that I'm late, but something came up.

LAVONDA. And it was *hard* for her to get away.

LATRELLE. Hi, Noleta.

NOLETA. Hey, Latrelle. Hey, Sissy.

SISSY. Hey, shug. *(Glances back at pad, mutters.)* Little people.

ROGER. It's always something.

   (**NOLETA** *rushes off stage.*)

NOLETA. *(Off stage.)* Oh, it was *something* alright.

LATRELLE. Well, I guess I missed whatever the something was. *(Calling.)* Noleta, could you fix my French manicure? And please focus this time.

   (**NOLETA** *rushes back in, pushing a manicure tray and pulling a rolling stool.*)

NOLETA. On it!

   (*She sits by* **LATRELLE** *and begins working on her nails.*)

LAVONDA. You've been missin' that something your entire life, Latrelle.

LATRELLE. Alley-cattin's never been my forte, unlike some.

LAVONDA. Hell's bells, Latrelle. My alley-cattin' years are a distant memory. And there was only one ol' cowboy that ever did anything for me in the first place. Shit, if it wadn't for my Rabbit, I'd never have another fuckin' orgasm in my fuckin' life. I'll buy you one for Christmas, Latrelle.

LATRELLE. Why wait? My birthday's next month.

LAVONDA. And this folks, is the perfect example that people can change. Sissy, you want a Rabbit?

SISSY. No ma'am. I do not like rodents.

ROGER. *(To* **LATRELLE.***)* Alright my dear, you are done!

(He turns the chair around, facing the mirror.)

LATRELLE. You are a miracle-worker, Roger!

*(**LATRELLE** gets up, grabs the hanging bag, exits to change.)*

*(Lights up sidewalk as **VERA**'s scooter travels across the apron of the stage; **VERA** driving, **MRS. BARNES** trotting behind. There is a cross placed on the basket, which is filled with anti-equality flyers and a hammer. They stop and nail an anti-equality revival flyer to a town bulletin board. In The Beehive, **LAVONDA** lights a cigarette and spots the duo through an imaginary "window".)*

LAVONDA. Oh, my god! I wish you would look at ol' Vera. I guess a life committed to riding a scooter is better than going on a diet!

(SISSY and ROGER light cigarettes and float over and watch through the "window". LAVONDA, ROGER and SISSY take drags simultaneously.)

Some people just don't care about their health.

(They exhale simultaneously, ROGER getting upset.)

SISSY. Vera has a disease, LaVonda.

ROGER. You know, I've got a good mind to go over and knock over that scooter and claw them to death with that fuckin' hammer then stuff those anti-equality signs down their throats!

SISSY. Roger, hun, you don't mean that! Murder is never a good option.

(VERA and MRS. BARNES head towards The Beehive.)

ROGER. I have just been beaten down all my life by the Bible, and at some point, there are no more cheeks to turn and no more fucks to give.

(SISSY digests this, as does LAVONDA. VERA enters the shop, followed by MRS. BARNES. SISSY, upset, gives ROGER a little hug.)

VERA. Ladies, it's so good that all of you are here together. We really want you to come to our revival.

(MRS. BARNES starts passing out the anti-equality flyers to everyone.)

LAVONDA. *(Mutters.)* Fuck that.

(LAVONDA throws the flyer in the trash as SISSY studies it for a moment, then looks at ROGER. She wads it up as she heads over to VERA.)

SISSY. Vera, I cannot be on your Anti-Equality Calling Committee.

MRS. BARNES. Sissy, you don't believe in equality, do you?

SISSY. I most certainly do.

> (**LATRELLE** *returns, now dressed in a low-cut, form-fitting dress. She walks over to* **NOLETA.**)

LATRELLE. *(Whispers.)* What's going on?

NOLETA. Sissy believes in equality now.

VERA. Well, then you don't believe the Bible. And, you're not right with your maker. Jesus spoke to us. He said no service to the gays. No cakes, no flowers, no photos and nobody to perform the weddings.

MRS. BARNES. No gay marriage in Winters, Texas! Ever, ever, ever!

SISSY. Shhhh. Jesus is speakin' to me, too. Right here and now. *(Closes her eyes.)* And the voice that I'm hearing is telling me –

MRS. BARNES. Speak to her, oh speak to her, Lord Jesus!

VERA. What? What's he saying?

SISSY. He's telling me that he never said dip to you and that you're a liar and a wolf in sheep's clothing!

LAVONDA. A very large sheep.

SISSY. *(Wheeling on* **LAVONDA.**) Stop your fat shaming, LaVonda! This has nothing to do with what's on the outside, but the awfulness inside these two hypocrites.

VERA. What has gotten into you, Sissy? You're hurtin' my feelin's.

> (**SISSY** *turns and stares at* **ROGER,** *who has tears in his eyes. She turns back to* **VERA.**)

SISSY. Love and compassion. Wasn't that Christ's real message? And now, I'm using my heart and the intelligence the good Lord give me to figure things out for myself.

VERA. Well, I'm not! *(Realizing.)* I didn't say that right.

LATRELLE. Oh, Vera, nothing you say is right.

SISSY. Come on, Latrelle, let's head over to San Angelo so we can tell your asshole ex-husband off, 'cause I'm on a roll. *(Notices LATRELLE's outfit.)* And, woo! You are ready! *(Pushes past VERA and MRS. BARNES.)* Get outta my way!

> *(SISSY and LATRELLE exit.)*

VERA. *(Calling after them).* Sinners!

> *(VERA catches herself in the mirror.)*

Oh, Roger hon, could you do a quick touch on our hair. I want to look my best for the revival tomorrow night.

> *(ROGER waves his rattail comb, gets in VERA's face.)*

ROGER. Get your bacon-eatin' Baptist asses out of my shop! And now that the Winter's Hairport is closed, and Lila Walker is no longer the oldest living beautician in the entire state of Texas because she is dead... who the fuck's gonna do your hair?! Yeah, bitches, anti-equality works both ways! Now you get the hell outta here before I beat you! Get out!

> *(ROGER grabs a handful of plastic rollers, starts throwing them as he chases the woman out of his shop. LAVONDA and NOLETA watch the chase, laughing as VERA and MRS. BARNES run out, followed by ROGER screaming, running, throwing rollers. Lights up on sidewalk as LAVONDA and NOLETA,*

laughing, follow **ROGER** *outside the shop, throwing rollers at* **VERA** *and* **MRS. BARNES**.)

Get out, get out, now! Get out, get out, now! That's right bitches, run, run! Get the fuck out!

(Terrified, **VERA** *gets on her scooter, takes off,* **MRS. BARNES** *trotting behind her,* **ROGER** *still on their asses,* **LAVONDA** *and* **NOLETA** *watching and laughing by The Beehive door.)*

Scoot, bitches, scoot!

MRS. BARNES. Who is going to do our hair?

ROGER. RUN!!!!!

(As the scooter, **VERA** *and* **MRS. BARNES** *exit,* **ROGER** *and* **LAVONDA** *high-five. As they exit with* **NOLETA**, *lights out on The Beehive.)*

Scene Eighteen

(*Cast:* **BROTHER BOY, BILLY JOE.**)

BROTHER BOY. (*Off stage, overlapping* **ROGER.**) Run!

> (**BROTHER BOY** *and* **BILLY JOE** *enter running across the apron.* **BROTHER BOY** *is carrying a make-up bag, a huge purse, a bag of clothes and a clear hanging bag with several costumes.*)

... Billy Joe, run! Run fast! That queen cannot be trusted. She's evil!

BILLY JOE. C'mon, c'mon. (*Points off stage.*) There's my truck!

> (**BROTHER BOY** *stumbles, drops some of his bags.*)

BROTHER BOY. Help me with this shit!

BILLY JOE. (*Turns.*) God, jeez, what is all that?

BROTHER BOY. It's my stuff, for my show.

> (**BILLY JOE** *grabs the bag of clothes and they continue on.*)

Now let's go!

> (**BILLY JOE** *exits.* **BROTHER BOY** *turns back.*)

Good-bye, Long-fuckin-view, Texas!

> (**BROTHER BOY** *turns to leave. Off stage a truck revs up.*)

(*As he exits.*) Haul ass, Billy Joe!

> (*The truck squeals, drives off.*)

> (*Blackout!*)

End of Act One

ACT TWO

Scene One

(Cast: **WARDELL, G.W., JUANITA, ODELL, JIMMY RAY, BILLY JOE, BROTHER BOY, TY, KYLE, ROGER.***)*

(In darkness, the strum of a guitar and intro to the **[SORDID LIVES REPRISE]**. *Spotlight hits* **WARDELL** *and the Bar Band in Bubba's Bar.)*

WARDELL. *(Singing.)*
NOW WHEN THE LORD DIPS US IN THE GENE POOL,
WE GET MORE THAN GRANNY'S GREEN EYES.

(Lights up truck. **BILLY JOE** *at the wheel, "driving";* **BROTHER BOY** *in the passenger's seat, primping in the "visor mirror".* **BILLY JOE** *glances over occasionally and smiles, amused.)*

(Singing.)

WE GET OUR MAMA'S WARMTH,
AND OUR DADDY'S COOL,
AND THAT THANG BETWEEN OUR THIGHS.

(Lights up on hotel room revealing **TY** *and* **KYLE**, *making love.)*

(Singing.)

THAT'S THE START OF ALL THESE TROUBLES,
IN OUR SORDID LIVES.

(Lights up church sign revealing **JIMMY RAY** *working on the new signage. The audience now sees that it reads: GOD LOVES GAYS BUT HE HATES PERVERTS. ROMANS 1: 26-27. ANTI-EQUALITY REVIVAL STARTS FRIDAY 7PM".* **JIMMY RAY** *finishes the job, stands back satisfied, gathers his letters and exits.)*

(Singing.)

AIN'T IT A BITCH.

G.W., ODELL & JUANITA. *(Yelling.)* Bitch.

WARDELL. *(Singing.)*
SORTIN' OUT OUR SORDID LIVES.
IT'S A BITCH.

G.W., ODELL & JUANITA. *(Yelling.)* Bitch.

WARDELL. *(Singing.)*
WHEN YOU COME TO REALIZE.

(Lights up on street as **ROGER** *walks across stage and spots the church sign. He rushes over and starts angrily rearranging the letters to read: GOD LOVES GAY BUTTS. He exits laughing.* **TY** *and* **KYLE** *make love to the rhythm of the song,* **BILLY JOE** *taps the steering wheel to the beat.)*

(Singing.)

WHEN YOU CRACK YOURSELF A BOX OF CRACKER JACK,
YOU CAN GET A REALLY SHITTY PRIZE.
IT'S A BITCH.

G.W., ODELL, JUANITA. *(Yelling.)* Bitch.

WARDELL. *(Singing.)*
SORTIN' OUT OUR SORRY LITTLE SORDID LIVES.

JUANITA. Amen! Praise Jesus!

(Lights out on all sets.)

Scene Two

(Cast: **BROTHER BOY, BILLY JOE, CASHIER.***)*

(Lights up on the truck as **BROTHER BOY** *and* **BILLY JOE** *continue to "drive",* **BROTHER BOY** *wearing the Tammy wig.)*

BROTHER BOY. So, do you prefer blondes?

(He then holds up the Loretta one.)

Or brunettes?

*(***BILLY JOE** *takes* **BROTHER BOY** *in.)*

BILLY JOE. I don't give a shit. So, where you wanna go?

BROTHER BOY. Dallas! To the Rose Room, where opportunity is rampant!

BILLY JOE. We're gonna need some money.

*(***BROTHER BOY** *rummages through his purse as* **BILLY JOE** *parks the truck, starts casing the joint.)*

I'll be right back. You stay put. Don't move.

BROTHER BOY. Would you be so kind to get me a Co-Cola?

BILLY JOE. What kind?

BROTHER BOY. Dr. Pepper. Oh, and some cigs. Eve Emerald Menthols, please. *(Pulls out a twenty dollar bill.)* Lord, I'm down to my last twenty. I shoulda grabbed that stash of tips.

BILLY JOE. Keep it. Don't need it.

*(***BILLY JOE** *gets out of the truck and strides towards the opposite side, exits.)*

BROTHER BOY. Well, what a gentleman.

(**BROTHER BOY** *adjusts the Tammy wig, freshens his lipstick, squirms a little, hums a little song, squirms some more.*)

I'm 'bout to bust my bladder.

(**BROTHER BOY** *gets out of the truck, sashays across the stage.*)

(Mutters.) He ain't the boss of me.

(Lights up convenience store. **BILLY JOE** *storms in, gun drawn, rushes to the counter, pointing the gun at a trembling* **CASHIER**.*)

BILLY JOE. Put all the fuckin' money in a fuckin' bag.

(**CASHIER** *empties the cash drawer in a paper bag as* **BROTHER BOY** *sees what is happening.*)

CASHIER. *(Overlap.)* Please don't kill me! Please! Take it all. I have a family, please just don't kill me.

BROTHER BOY. *(Overlap.)* Oh my stars and stripes!

BILLY JOE. *(Overlap).* All the money in that fuckin' bag! That's it, right there. Give me the fuckin' money! Give me the fuckin' money, or I'll shoot you in the fucking face!

BROTHER BOY. I might have bit off more than I can chew.

(**BILLY JOE** *grabs the bag of money and flees, sees* **BROTHER BOY**, *grabs his arm and they run to the truck.*)

BILLY JOE. Get in the truck!

(**CASHIER** *rushes out, now carrying a pistol, starts firing.*)

BROTHER BOY. Oh! Oh! Oh! They're shootin' at us! Zigzag Billy Joe, zigzag!

BILLY JOE. Get in the truck! Get in the goddamn truck!!!

(They get in the truck.)

BROTHER BOY. Well, if I'd known you was gonna commit armed robbery, I would *not* have worn my kitten heels!

BILLY JOE. Let's go!

(Sound effect of tires screeching and a bullet hitting metal, as they speed off. Lights out on the truck.)

Scene Three

(Cast: **LAVONDA, NOLETA, AUNT LITTLE NEECY** *(Off stage),* **HARDY, NURSE SAMPLE.***)*

(Lights up on a hospital hallway. **LAVONDA** *and* **NOLETA** *walk with purpose.)*

LAVONDA. Hurry up! I don't want Aunt Little Neecy to see me. She's become attached.

> *(***HARDY** *enters, coming the other way, on crutches, now in sweats,* **NURSE SAMPLE** *helping him. They walk towards* **NOLETA** *and* **LAVONDA.** *He flashes a flirty smile as he reaches* **NOLETA.***)*

HARDY. *(Leans in to* **NOLETA.***)* Did you miss me?

NOLETA. Well, kinda.

HARDY. I'm not wearing any underwear.

> *(***NURSE SAMPLE** *shoots* **HARDY** *a dirty look, then stares at his package.)*

LAVONDA. *(Clears her throat.)* Your mama.

NOLETA. Oh, right. Tests pending are no longer pending.

HARDY. *(Smiles, moves closer.)* Well, if it's bad news, you come back here and I will comfort you, but if it's good news you come back here and we'll celebrate.

NOLETA. Win-win.

HARDY. Yeah.

> *(***HARDY** *and* **NURSE SAMPLE** *travel on.)*

LAVONDA. How the fuck is this happening to you?

NURSE SAMPLE. Trash.

> *(Lights out on hallway.)*

Scene Four

(Cast: **SISSY, LATRELLE, GRETA, WILSON.***)*

(Lights up on **LATRELLE***'s former mini-mansion as* **LATRELLE** *and* **SISSY** *arrive at the door.* **LATRELLE** *stops, adjusts her blouse to expose more cleavage.)*

LATRELLE. How do I look?

SISSY. Like you are not going to church.

*(***LATRELLE** *takes a deep breath, rings the doorbell. A moment before* **GRETA***, late 20s, dressed in Daisy Dukes and a tube top opens the door. Her face drops when she sees* **LATRELLE.***)*

GRETA. Ugh. What the hell do you want?

LATRELLE. *(Giving her the once-over.)* Hello Greta. I need to speak to Wilson.

GRETA. Have you ever heard of the telephone or email?

LATRELLE. Have you ever heard of age-appropriate dressing?

GRETA. Whatever. *(Mutters.)* Bitch. *(Calls into the house.)* Wilson! Your ex-wife Latrene is here!

LATRELLE. Latrelle! You know it's Latrelle.

*(***WILSON***,* **LATRELLE***'s ex-husband,* **TY***'s Dad, appears at the door. He is in sweaty workout clothes, is orange from fake tanning, with overly dyed hair, trying way too hard.)*

WILSON. What the hell do you want?

LATRELLE. *(To* **GRETA.***)* Do you mind?

WILSON. Whatever you have to say to me, you can say in front of my wife.

LATRELLE. Wife?

(**GRETA** *sticks her hand out, showing off a huge diamond.*)

GRETA. That's right! Wife! Right after my divorce was final last month and we were both free of our horrible past, we had a simple, private ceremony in San Antonio with a mariachi band. It was perfect for our simple, yet pure, love.

LATRELLE. *(Stunned.)* Well, I... I didn't know.

WILSON. Well, what'd you expect, Latrelle? A wedding invitation?

(**WILSON** *and* **GRETA** *laugh.*)

LATRELLE. *(Blurting out.)* You're gonna be a grandpa, Wilson!

WILSON. What?

LATRELLE. Ty and Kyle's surrogate is pregnant with twins.

SISSY. I can explain how that works if y'all need me to.

WILSON. Works against God's nature is what it does just as their relationship and their lifestyle works against God's will.

GRETA. That's right, we believe that God created Adam and Eve, not Adam and Steve, and that marriage is between a man and a woman.

LATRELLE. Shouldn't that be between a man, his first wife, and then a couple of trashy waitresses?

GRETA. *(To* **WILSON.***)* Did she just call me trashy?

LATRELLE. Well, if the hooker heel fits.

(**SISSY** *giggles.*)

GRETA. And I am a singer, not a waitress!

LATRELLE. At the Bowl-a-rama!

GRETA. Wilson, are you going to allow her talk to me like this?

LATRELLE. Allow? Oh honey, he never had that kind of control over me!

(**SISSY** *digs in her purse, pulls out her Bible.*)

SISSY. Greta, hun, do y'all believe all the Bible?

GRETA. *(A desperate look to* **WILSON.***)* This feels like a trick question?

WILSON. We absolutely do! We hate the sin, but we love the sinner.

SISSY. Latrelle, we're gonna need some rocks.

GRETA. Rocks?

SISSY. Yes, hun, I hate to inform you, but the Bible is very clear on stonin' adulterers. Covered in several passages. So I guess me and Latrelle are gonna have to stone you and Wilson. Ooh! Would over there in the driveway be acceptable?

LATRELLE. *(Indicating.)* Sissy, would these bricks that I lined this flower bed with... will they do?

WILSON. Get off of my property!

LATRELLE. *(In* **WILSON***'s face.)* You are gonna be a grandpa, Wilson! Our *gay* son is going to be a daddy and he will parent with the *gay* man who he loves and is legally married to! So, get used to it and stop being such a terrible father!

WILSON. Get off my property!

GRETA. Yeah! Or I'm gonna call the police.

LATRELLE. The property that you stole from me? Gladly! Come on Sissy!

> (**LATRELLE** *walks away.* **SISSY** *rushes up to* **GRETA.***)*

SISSY. Nice to meet you, Greta. I am real happy we didn't have to stone you. *(Fake smile.)* Wilson.

> (*Lights out on the mini mansion as* **WILSON** *and* **GRETA** *exit. Lights up on a driveway as* **SISSY** *catches up to* **LATRELLE.***)*

Good job, Latrelle.

LATRELLE. I felt that went well.

> (*Sound effect of* **LATRELLE**'*s phone receiving a text message.* **LATRELLE** *pulls out her phone, stops, reads it.*)

Oh, Sissy, look! My grandbabies.

> (*She hands* **SISSY** *her phone.* **SISSY** *stares.*)

SISSY. Awwwww. They look like little aliens. *(Turns the phone over.)* I wonder which one is the mixed twin?

> (**LATRELLE** *takes the phone back and dials, stares at her former home.*)

LATRELLE. Ty, they're precious! Just precious. *(Emotional.)* I need you to come home. Winters needs you. I need you.

> (*Lights out on driveway.*)

Scene Five

(Cast: **NOLETA, HARDY, LAVONDA, NURSE SAMPLE.***)*

(In darkness.)

NOLETA. I am so glad it was ptomaine and not cancer!

HARDY. The lord works in mysterious ways!

> *(Lights up on hospital room #2.* **NOLETA** *and* **HARDY** *are now in the bed, going at it;* **NOLETA** *is on top, riding* **HARDY.***)*

NOLETA. Oh yes he does! Oh give glory, give glory!

> *(Lights up on hospital hallway.* **LAVONDA** *enters going one way,* **NURSE SAMPLE** *enters going the other. They both stop when they hear:)*

HARDY. Hallelujah!

NOLETA. Oh, Jesus!

HARDY. Ahhhh!

NOLETA. Win! Win! Win, win, win, WIN! *(Pauses.)* Hold on, one, one more!

LAVONDA. Noleta?

NOLETA. Ahhhh! WIN! JEEEEE-SUS! Win, win, win!

> *(***NURSE SAMPLE** *is appalled and turned on simultaneously, touching her breast.* **LAVONDA** *exchanges a look with* **NURSE SAMPLE,** *who stops massaging herself.)*

NURSE SAMPLE. Trash.

> *(***NURSE SAMPLE** *and* **LAVONDA** *exit as lights out on hospital hallway and hospital room.)*

Scene Six

(Cast: **TY, KYLE.***)*

(Lights up on a hotel room as **TY** *and* **KYLE***'s love making heats up. Hot and sexy.)*

TY. Who's your Daddy?

KYLE. You are! Give it to me, Daddy!

*(***TY*** suddenly starts laughing.)*

What?

TY. I'm sorry. I think we have to come up with a better way to talk dirty. I don't think we can use "Daddy" like that anymore.

KYLE. *(Laughing.)* Right. Wow. We're gonna be daddies, Ty.

TY. And we're going to be the best damn daddies God ever put on this earth. *(Mood change.)* Unlike mine.

KYLE. Hey, you're bringing us down. *(Looks under sheet.)* Literally. Talk dirty, baby.

(They start kissing again.)

TY. *(Struggling.)* Um, give me that BBC my um... hot black man?

KYLE. *(Laughing.)* That's the best you can do? Pathetic!

(They enjoy the laugh. As the passion ignites again, lights out hotel room.)

Scene Seven

(Cast: **SISSY, LAVONDA, T.V. NEWSCASTER** *(Voice over).)*

(Lights up on **SISSY***'s house.* **SISSY** *watches TV and smokes.* **LAVONDA** *enters with a stack of pictures, goes to end table and grabs another one, during:)*

TV NEWSCASTER VOICE. *(On TV.)* In other news, Texas Attorney General Ken Paxton is telling county officials that they can deny marriage licenses to same-sex couples if they have religious objections to doing so.

SISSY. Sore losers if you ask me. *(Mutes TV.)* Why're you takin' all my pictures of your mama?

LAVONDA. Wardell wants me to bring some over to Bubba's for Mama's memorial service.

SISSY. Awwww. *(Notices TV, unmutes.)* Oh, oh, breaking news!

TV NEWSCASTER VOICE. *(On TV.)* And breaking news just into our news room, The Hitchhiker Murderer, Billy Joe Dobson, is still on the loose, but he was spotted today in what appears to be the kidnapping of an elderly woman.

*(***LAVONDA** *and* **SISSY** *study the TV.)*

LAVONDA. You know, that hostage looks vaguely familiar.

(Lights out on **SISSY***'s house.)*

Scene Eight

(Cast: **BROTHER BOY, BILLY JOE.***)*

(Lights up on a seedy motel room. **BROTHER BOY** *sits in a chair, staring at a very naked* **BILLY JOE.** *A neon light effect flashes through the window.)*

BROTHER BOY. Kinda looks like a bald, naked Jesus if Jesus had tattoos, which he did not.

*(***BILLY JOE** *stirs.)*

BILLY JOE. Who the hell are you talking to?

BROTHER BOY. You. Just a silly way of waking you up. Beats the hell out of... *(Singing.)*
"RISE AND SHINE AND GIVE GOD THE GLORY, GLORY."

BILLY JOE. Dude, you are fucking crazy. And I like crazy.

BROTHER BOY. How long we gotta hide out here?

BILLY JOE. Just a couple of hours 'til it's dark... let things cool down, then we'll take the back roads on up to Dallas.

BROTHER BOY. This life of crime is so exciting! I love being on the lam with you in a stolen vehicle! Just like Bonnie and Clyde. Let's just not get shot dead, shall we?

*(***BROTHER BOY** *giggles, then stops when* **BILLY JOE** *just stares and smiles, shakes his head.)*

Why don't you scare me?

BILLY JOE. I think my killin' days are over. Maybe you can sense that.

BROTHER BOY. Well, that certainly works in my favor.

BILLY JOE. Come over here by me.

*(BROTHER BOY does. BILLY JOE moves into
BROTHER BOY's lap, covers his naked body up
to his waist.)*

You mind?

BROTHER BOY. No, uh-uh, I don't mind.

BILLY JOE. See... the killing was all connected to sex. I'm
attracted to women and men, just about everything.
Except farm animals. But, my attraction is only for
dead people. 'Sides, I can't get this monster dick of
mine up no more. Them days are over.

BROTHER BOY. Monster?

(BILLY JOE lifts the sheet to prove his point.)

BILLY JOE. Uh-huh.

BROTHER BOY. *(Studies it.)* Where does it end? *(BILLY JOE
lifts higher.)* You may be a killer, but you ain't a liar.

BILLY JOE. *(Mood change.)* I didn't wanna be that. A killer.
And I take full responsibility, but I had a childhood
that was like a goddamn horror movie. Can't go there.
It was just somethin' ...the killin' ... I couldn't control.
I tried. So hard. My kind ain't too popular in the big
house. Some inmates cut my nuts off.

BROTHER BOY. Cut your nuts off?

BILLY JOE. Yup. Them guards just stood back and laughed,
almost bled to death. If it hadn't been for this big ol'
black queer named Rib-Eye, I woulda. Maybe that's
why I like you. You kinda remind me of ol' Rib-Eye.

BROTHER BOY. You've lost me.

BILLY JOE. Well, he was real, real sissy, almost a woman.

BROTHER BOY. Oh, yeah, well, that makes complete sense.

BILLY JOE. But Rib-Eye saved my life, sewed my nut sack
shut, hurt like a motherfucker, then nursed me back

to health, real tender-like. I felt more love than I had ever felt in my life. He didn't want sex... nothing... just love. But, then Rib Eye met his maker. Got into some bad drug shit and was stabbed, right in front of me. *(Pause, emotional.)* Everybody I ever love just leaves. I'm scared to die. 'Cause, I know with all I done here on this earth, I don't have no chance of going to heaven. I will be burning in that lake of fire for eternity. Bound for hell. So, that's why I escaped 'cause they was supposed to execute me in a few days and I was scared shitless.

(**BILLY JOE** *gets up, slides up by* **BROTHER BOY**.)

So, I guess, in a way, losing my nuts was the best thing that coulda happened to me. And you. 'Cause if I still had my nuts, I'da killed you, and then we'd have sex... which you couldn't enjoy 'cause you would be dead, but then I'd certainly be attracted to you.

BROTHER BOY.   Well, thank you... that helps. I suffer from low self-esteem. *(Pause.)* Dear sweet Jesus, this is the strangest conversation I have ever had in my entire life.

(**BILLY JOE** *stares at* **BROTHER BOY**.)

What?

(**BILLY JOE** *leans in and kisses* **BROTHER BOY**, *sweet, caring.*)

BILLY JOE.   For Rib Eye.

(Lights out on seedy motel room.)

Scene Nine

(*Cast:* **G.W., ODELL, JUANITA, WARDELL, LAVONDA.***)*

(*Lights up on Bubba's Bar as we find the trio of drunks sitting on their perches, heads down, passed out.* **WARDELL** *tries to take* **JUANITA***'s beer from her. She holds tight, takes a final, long swig, eyes still closed, then releases it to* **WARDELL** *as she puts her head back down. Soft country music in style of Buck Owens'* ["**TOGETHER AGAIN**"] *scores the scene as* **LAVONDA** *enters, carrying the pictures of* **PEGGY***. She pauses by the door, smiles as she watches* **WARDELL** *take the keys away from* **G.W.** *and* **ODELL***.*)

LAVONDA. Still takin' away keys and drivin' all the drunks home, huh?

WARDELL. Keeps me in business.

LAVONDA. You're a good man, Wardell.

WARDELL. Well, hell.

(**LAVONDA** *walks over to* **WARDELL** *and lays the pictures down.*)

LAVONDA. Looky what I found.

---

* A license to produce A VERY SORDID WEDDING does not include a performance license for "TOGETHER AGAIN". The publisher and author suggest that the licensee contact ASCAP or BMI to ascertain the music publisher and contact such music publisher to license or acquire permission for performance of the song. If a license or permission is unattainable for "TOGETHER AGAIN", the licensee may not use the song in A VERY SORDID WEDDING but should create an original composition in a similar style or use a similar song in the public domain. For further information, please see Music Use Note on page 3.

*(She holds up one picture. **WARDELL** takes it.
Their hands touch for moment.)*

WARDELL. I remember that day like it was yesterday.

LAVONDA. Lord! Look how young we were.

WARDELL. Yeah, that was about the time that I kissed the most beautiful gal I'd ever laid eyes on, down by the old cow pond.

LAVONDA. Oh, that's not all we did down by the cow pond, if I remember correctly. I was barely sixteen. Ah, young love, nothing like it.

> *(**WARDELL** puts down the picture, pulls **LAVONDA** closer.)*

WARDELL. Well, maybe there is, Vonie. 'Cause you're still the most beautiful gal I've ever laid eyes on.

> *(**WARDELL** takes **LAVONDA**'s face in his hands and kisses her. A kiss that has been waiting to happen for many, many years.)*

I never stopped lovin' you, Vonie.

LAVONDA. I never stopped lovin' you, Wardell.

> *(They kiss again, then as emotion grips both of them, **WARDELL** pulls **LAVONDA** closer, and they dance. **JUANITA** wakes up, lights up, then opens her purse, pulls out a tube of lipstick and a compact. **JUANITA** reapplies her lipstick to one side of her lips, then moves her cigarette, never taking it from her lips, and completes the job.)*

JUANITA. Hey! Do y'all still think I'm pretty?

> *(**WARDELL** and **LAVONDA**, dance on as lights fade on Bubba's Bar.)*

Scene Ten

(Cast: **BROTHER BOY, BILLY JOE.***)*

(Lights up on truck. **BILLY JOE** *pulls up, stops.*
BROTHER BOY *in passenger's seat, looks at
him sadly as they arrive at their destination.)*

BILLY JOE. Well, this is it.

BROTHER BOY. The Rose Room! Where drag queens'
dreams come true. Oh Lord, I'm as nervous as a
pregnant nun.

BILLY JOE. You got this. You were born to perform. Now go
in there and knock 'em dead.

BROTHER BOY. *(Giggles.)* Knock 'em dead. Oh, the irony.
(Gets emotional.) I'm gonna miss you, Billy Joe.

BILLY JOE. *(Fighting emotion.)* Yeah, I'm... well... okay...
get out!

BROTHER BOY. You deserved a better life.

> **(BILLY JOE** *reaches under the seat, grabs the
> bag of money, hands it to* **BROTHER BOY.***)*

BILLY JOE. You're gonna need this. Plenty more where that
came from.

BROTHER BOY. Thank you, Billy Joe. I learned something
very valuable from meetin' you.

BILLY JOE. What's that?

BROTHER BOY. *(Sincere.)* Never judge a serial killer. Bye,
bye.

> **(BROTHER BOY** *quickly kisses* **BILLY JOE** *on
> the cheek, then gets out of the truck with his
> belongings and the bag of money. Lights
> out truck. Lights up street as* **BROTHER BOY**

is drawn to the thump thump of music. He looks out towards the audience as if he's reading a sign, a neon light effect flashing over his face.)

The Rose Room. *(Reading.)* Amateur drag competition. Tonight! It's a sign!

*(**BROTHER BOY** smiles, takes a deep breath, gathers all his belonging, looks up and smiles.)*

(Lights out on street.)

Scene Eleven

(*Cast:* **BROTHER BOY, CASSIE NOVA, EDNA JEAN ROBINSON, PETER, DRAG QUEEN** *extras,* **TY, KYLE, ROSE ROOM ANNOUNCER** (*Voice over*).)

(*Lights up on the rose room.* **BROTHER BOY** *enters to find* **CASSIE NOVA,** *a fierce* **DRAG QUEEN** *in a big, red wig signing up amateur contestants for the competition and* **EDNA JEAN ROBINSON,** *an older church lady* **DRAG QUEEN,** *mingling.* **PETER,** *a hard-bodied, hot, shot boy, clad only in Andrew Christian underwear, combat boots and maybe a cap, approaches* **BROTHER BOY** *as he sets down his drag clothes and suitcases, looking around in awe.*)

PETER. You moving in?

BROTHER BOY. No, I'm not moving in, I just wanted choices for the competition.

(**BROTHER BOY** *fixates on* **PETER***'s big bulge, points.*)

Oh, your Andrew Christians are, woo, not real Christian. (*Looks around with nervous excitement.*) Ah! The Rose Room! I'm just, I'm overwhelmed.

(**PETER** *hands a shot to* **BROTHER BOY.**)

PETER. Need a shot of courage?

BROTHER BOY. Yeah, I'm nervous.

(**BROTHER BOY** *pulls a twenty from his bag of money, hands it to* **PETER,** *then downs the shot.*)

Keep it and keep 'em comin'. I'll need many, many more!

> (**EDNA JEAN** *wanders over, picks up the hanging bag, takes a couple of gowns out.*)

EDNA JEAN. Girl, I love this dress. And this one is divine!

BROTHER BOY. I made it myself.

EDNA JEAN. Shut the front door! You're gonna be fabulous, baby.

BROTHER BOY. Well thank yewwww!

EDNA JEAN. Come with me, let's get you signed up.

> (**PETER** *hands* **BROTHER BOY** *another shot. He downs it, then heads over to* **CASSIE**.)

CASSIE NOVA. Grandmother? Did they let you out of the home? Edna Jean, sign up Angie Dickinson here.

> (**EDNA JEAN** *hands* **BROTHER BOY** *a clipboard.*)

EDNA JEAN. Just sign your real name there, your drag name right there. And don't pay any attention to Cassie. She's bipolar. I think you're a beautiful cupcake covered in sprinkles in a world full of bran muffins.

CASSIE NOVA. Does anybody have a barf bag?

BROTHER BOY. *(To* **CASSIE NOVA**.*)* I'm not Angie Dickinson. I am Tammy Wynette.

CASSIE NOVA. More like Tammy Why Not!

> (**BROTHER BOY** *signs up.* **PETER** *passes by again.* **BROTHER BOY** *grabs a shot from his tray as* **CASSIE** *exits.*)

BROTHER BOY. That big red one is vicious.

PETER. Wait 'til you hear this audience.

EDNA JEAN. Girl, come with me. Let's get you ready!

> (**BROTHER BOY** *downs the shot, then another.*
> **EDNA JEAN** *leads* **BROTHER BOY** *off stage as*
> **TY** *and* **KYLE** *rush in, holding hands, ready*
> *for a gay night out in Dallas.*)

TY. Time to celebrate my baby's new job! And before we go back to Winters, I need a drink – or six. *(Looks around.)* Oh god, this is where I learned to be gay.

KYLE. Under what table?

TY. All of them!

> (**TY** *and* **KYLE** *sit at a high top as lights dim.*
> *Drum roll.*)

ROSE ROOM ANNOUNCER. Ladies and gentleman, please welcome to the stage, the mouth of the South – Cassie Nova!

> (**CASSIE NOVA** *struts on stage, spotlight hits*
> *her.*)

CASSIE NOVA. Hey all you crazy motherfuckers! Welcome, welcome, welcome to the amateur show tonight here at the Rose Room at S4! Y'all, get ready to support... and make fun of... 'cause I know that's why some of you are here tonight!

> (*A* **TRAGIC DRAG QUEEN** *enters.*)

CASSIE. And some girl are just flat-out tragic! *(Re:* **TRAGIC QUEEN**.*)* Eeww. Makes me wanna drink. Y'all wanna do a shot with me? *(Motions for* **PETER**.*)* Come here, baby. Y'all say hello to Peter. *(Leans down, waves at his bulge.)* Hey, Peter. *(Takes a shot, toasts audience.)* Now lift your glass with me. In the name of the Lord and all that is holy, cheers to queers! And for you cheap fuckers, don't forget to tip your bartenders, servers, queens and most importantly – me! Now, let's get this train wreck... um, show on the road! Edna Jean, is that old one ready?

EDNA. *(Peaking in.)* As she's gonna get.

CASSIE. For our first entertainer, I want y'all to keep y'all's expectations real low because this old cunt-try queen is tired as fuck. Ladies and gentlemen, Miss Tammy Why Not!

EDNA JEAN. *(Enters, calls offstage.)* You're up, sister.

> *(**BROTHER BOY** enters as **PETER** approaches. **BROTHER BOY** grabs one more shot as a song in the style of Tammy Wynette's [**"WOMANHOOD"**]* starts playing.)*

BROTHER BOY. It's Wynette. Run tell her. Tammy Wynette.

> *(**BROTHER BOY** downs the shot, is now obviously drunk, and he weaves to center stage. A spotlight hits him, blinding him like a deer in headlights. He starts lipsyncing badly.)*

EDNA JEAN. Oh dear gay Jesus –!

> *(And it only gets worse. **KYLE** and **TY** in audience watch in sympathy.)*

KYLE. Bless her heart.

TY. Come on, old girl!

---

* A license to produce A VERY SORDID WEDDING does not include a performance license for "WOMANHOOD". The publisher and author suggest that the licensee contact ASCAP or BMI to ascertain the music publisher and contact such music publisher to license or acquire permission for performance of the song. If a license or permission is unattainable for "WOMANHOOD", the licensee may not use the song in A VERY SORDID WEDDING but should create an original composition in a similar style or use a similar song in the public domain. For further information, please see Music Use Note on page 3.

(**BROTHER BOY** *tries adding a little choreography. A tragic mistake. He stumbles and falls, an audience member yanks off his wig, then throws it to Tragic Drag Queen who throws it to* **TY.***)*

BROTHER BOY. *(Overlap.)* That's my hair! I can't perform without my hair on!

(*The music continues blaring, everybody laughing as* **BROTHER BOY** *staggers off the stage.*)

TY. *(Realizing.)* I think that was my Uncle Brother Boy.

(**TY** *takes the wig, grabs* **KYLE***'s hand and they rush off to find* **BROTHER BOY** *as* **CASSIE** *returns to the stage.*)

CASSIE NOVA. I don't think she's gonna win.

(*Lights out on the* **ROSE ROOM.***)*

Scene Twelve

(Cast: **BROTHER BOY, TY, KYLE***)*

(Lights up the **ROSE ROOM** *dressing room.* **BROTHER BOY** *sits at a makeup table, his bag of clothes and gowns by it, sobbing.)*

BROTHER BOY. *(Looks up.)* Oh, my precious, precious, precious Tammy. I have betrayed your memory and did not carry on your legacy! *(More tears.)* I am so very sorry.

> *(***TY** *and* **KYLE** *enter.* **BROTHER BOY** *looks up as* **TY** *hands him the wig.)*

Thank you. George Jones drank to calm his nerves. It did not work for me.

TY. Excuse me, but –

BROTHER BOY. I'm sorry y'all had to witness this catastrophe. I got on stage, and I just bunched up. My throat, I just... I couldn't. I froze.

TY. I think you're my Uncle Brother Boy.

BROTHER BOY. *(Evaluates* **TY***, realizes.)* You're Latrelle's boy?

TY. I am.

BROTHER BOY. Ty.

TY. Yes. And this is my husband, Kyle.

BROTHER BOY. Your husband? *(Chokes up.)* Oh, I could just weep. I just want to kiss you on the cheek... both of ya.

> *(He rises and kisses* **TY***, then* **KYLE***.)*

KYLE. I love those nails.

BROTHER BOY. They'd look good with your beautiful complexion.

TY. Do you live here?

BROTHER BOY. Nuh-uh. I hitchhiked up here from Longview with... it's just a really long story. *(Points to his belongings.)* Everything I own is in a sack. All my possessions, my worldly possessions, are in a sack.

TY. We're headed back to Winters, Uncle Brother Boy. Do you want to come home with us?

BROTHER BOY. Hell no! I hadn't been home since I saw you last time at Mama's funeral. That was almost a bigger nightmare than tonight.

TY. I think you should reconsider. It's time we all be a family again.

> *(Lights out on the* **ROSE ROOM** *dressing room as* **TY** *and* **BROTHER BOY** *hug again.)*

Scene Thirteen

(Cast: **SISSY, LAVONDA, TY, KYLE, BROTHER BOY,** T.V. **NEWSCASTER** *(Voice over),* **LATRELLE, NOLETA.***)*

(Lights up on **SISSY***'s house.* **SISSY** *dusts, cigarette dangling from her lips.)*

SISSY. *(Singing.)*
"ARE YOU WARSHED, IN THE BLOOD? IN THE SOUL CLEANSIN' BLOOD OF THE LAMB. ARE YOUR GARMENTS SPOTLESS, ARE THEY ..."

*(***LAVONDA** *enters sheepishly.)*

Speaking of garments. The walk of shame. You hussy!

LAVONDA. Guilty!

SISSY. Where have you been all night?

LAVONDA. Oh, Sissy, me and Wardell got back together!

SISSY. Awww! I'm so happy for you!

(They squeal and hug as the doorbell rings.)

Well, who in the world?

LAVONDA. You expecting anybody?

*(***SISSY** *answers the door.)*

SISSY. Ty! Oh, heavens to Betsy! Ty! Come on in! LaVonda, Ty's here!

*(***SISSY** *ushers* **TY** *in, followed by* **KYLE. TY** *hugs* **SISSY.** *Lots of overlaps as they greet.)*

TY. Aunt Sissy!

*(***SISSY** *then goes to* **KYLE** *as* **LAVONDA** *rushes* **TY.***)*

LAVONDA. *(Screaming as they hug.)* Ty!!!

TY. Hello, favorite aunt of mine!

SISSY. And you must be Kyle! Welcome to Winters!

> *(**SISSY** hugs **KYLE**.)*

KYLE. It's a pleasure to be here.

TY. And, look who we found just wandering the streets of Dallas!

> *(**BROTHER BOY** struts in wearing casual drag as **LAVONDA** hugs **KYLE**.)*

SISSY. Oh, sweet baby Jesus! Brother Boy!

> *(She hugs him and squeals.)*

BROTHER BOY. Hey, Sissy!

> *(**LAVONDA** screams with excitement upon seeing **BROTHER BOY**, goes to hug him.)*

Hey LaVonda, I finally made it! I made it!

SISSY. Everybody come on in! Sit down and let's visit and catch up! What a wonderful surprise!

LAVONDA. *(Tearfully hugging **BROTHER BOY**.)* It is so good to see you!

> *(**SISSY** suddenly notices something on the TV, grabs the remote and unmutes it.)*

SISSY. Shh, shh.

TV NEWSCASTER VOICE. *(On TV.)* We interrupt this program for this breaking news. We have an update on the Hitchhiker Murderer. Billy Joe Dobson is dead.

> *(**BROTHER BOY** gasps and tears fill his eyes.)*

SISSY. Good!

TV NEWSCASTER VOICE. *(On TV.)* The escaped serial killer was killed during a shootout with police after a dramatic car chase through Dallas late last night. Take a close look here, this elderly woman is believed to be The Hitchhiker Murderer's final victim.

BROTHER BOY. Elderly.

TV NEWSCASTER VOICE. *(On TV.)* Police are currently looking for her body. We will keep you updated as we learn more.

BROTHER BOY. *(Through emotion.)* A fallen angel has returned to heaven.

SISSY. Yes, she has. That poor old woman. Wonder why she was hitchhiking at her age?

LATRELLE. *(Screaming off stage.)* Sissy! Sissy!

> *(**LATRELLE** comes flying in the front door.
> **BROTHER BOY** retreats in the corner so she
> doesn't see him.)*

Sissy!!! *(She spots **TY**.)* Ty! You made it!

> *(They hug.)*

TY. We did! We made it, Mama!

LATRELLE. *(Hugging **KYLE**.)* Kyle! *(To all.)* Oh... well, good! I got everything planned. It's all mapped out.

TY. Look who we brought.

> *(**TY** points at **BROTHER BOY**. **LATRELLE** turns,
> stares, emotion consuming her.)*

LATRELLE. Brother Boy. *(Studies him.)* You look... very pretty. I missed you.

> *(She walks over to him.)*

BROTHER BOY. Do I know you?

LATRELLE. I guess I deserved that, but I'm trying.

LAVONDA. Oh, she's still a bitch. But, it's just not nonstop anymore.

LATRELLE. *(Sharply.)* Do you mind?!

Brother Boy, I was awful to you. For years. And I'm so sor –

BROTHER BOY. Honey, you don't have to do this –

LATRELLE. No, no, I need to. I'm sorry. It's just that so much has changed. Is changing. Guess it just took me a while.

BROTHER BOY. A while?

LATRELLE. Too long, okay? I want to make up for lost time. Can we? Can we go back to the way it was when we were little, when we used to play dress-up together?

BROTHER BOY. *(Looks* **LATRELLE** *up and down.)* What size dress you wearing these days?

> *(***LATRELLE** *laughs, then opens her arms and they hug.)*

LATRELLE. Oh, I love you. I love you!

BROTHER BOY. I love you, too, Latrelle. *(Chuckles.)* Good lord.

> *(***NOLETA** *rushes in, stops in her tracks when she spots* **KYLE***.)*

NOLETA. Oh, he *is* black!

KYLE. I prefer hot chocolate mocha.

TY. Venti, of course.

SISSY. Has Hot Chocolate Mocha replaced African-American?

KYLE. Naw, I'm just being silly. *(Stands.)* And I'm guessing this pretty lady must be Noleta.

NOLETA. Why, thank you. Yes, Noleta. I'm white. Can't even tan. And I'm in love, too. I think. But it's not the gay love. Can't go there. Sometimes I think it'd be easier, less complicated, but I am attracted to black men –

> *(SISSY smacks her arm.)*

Oww... um, uh, African-American men. Sorry.

KYLE. Black works. I've never been to Africa.

SISSY. Well, I sure am excited about... *(Focusing hard to get it right.)* ...your one white and one mixed twin.

TY. We prefer biracial.

SISSY. Biracial. Oh, Lord, I cannot keep up.

> *(SISSY reaches for her pad and pen, opens it and starts to write. KYLE glances at it, gently takes it.)*

KYLE. Girl, you been busy!

SISSY. I try. I do my best.

KYLE. And that's what matters. I believe the intention is more important than the words.

LATRELLE. All good to know, but we gotta get organized for the anti-equality revival tonight. We gotta get busy. Because shit is about to hit the fan!

> *(Lights out on SISSY's house.)*

Scene Fourteen

(Cast: **VERA, NURSE SAMPLE, MRS. BARNES, JUANITA, EXTRA ANTI-EQUALITY MEMBERS.***)*

(Lights up on The Corner Stop. **VERA** *sits on her stool, now in front of her counter. Her hair is a mess.* **NURSE SAMPLE** *works on her hair with* **MRS. BARNES,** *also in desperate need of a hair appointment, working on* **NURSE SAMPLE***'s hair. A couple of other anti-equality members (if available) do the same. A chain gang of sorts.)*

VERA. Ladies, thank you for coming to our final Anti-Equality Committee meeting before the big revival tonight.

MRS. BARNES. Hold still, sweetie. There's a hole in the back of your hair as big as Houston that I'm trying to cover.

NURSE SAMPLE. Ouch! I'm tender headed! Roger never hurts me! This is not working. We look like wet cats!

VERA. Roger is just a hateful-hearted homosexual who will pay for this by going straight to hell! *(Then sweetly.)* Sister Barnes, please lead us in an opening word of prayer.

MRS. BARNES. Well, of course. Ladies. *(They stand and all join hands.)* Dear Heavenly Father, we gather here today in thy presence before our anti-equality revival tonight. We pray for the soul of Sissy Hickey who now believes in equality. We pray for Latrelle Williamson who called our dear Vera a glutton. Let the church house be packed to the rafters, oh Lord!

NURSE SAMPLE. Yes, Lord!

MRS. BARNES. Let sinners walk in that front door!

(JUANITA staggers in the store, takes in the scene.)

JUANITA. What's going on here!?

NURSE SAMPLE. Juanita, hon, we're right in the middle of our final Anti-Equality Committee meeting.

JUANITA. That doesn't sound right.

MRS. BARNES. Well, it is! Now, we would just love for you to come tonight as we stop equality from infiltrating Runnels County.

JUANITA. I have a conflict. There's something going on real important over at that bar that I sometimes frequent, uh, called uh... I forget.

VERA. Bubba's?

JUANITA. That would be the one.

NURSE SAMPLE. Might as well be called "The Den of Iniquity".

JUANITA. I think that one's over in New Orleans.

(JUANITA grabs a bag of Cheetos from the chip stand. Tosses them on the counter.)

(To VERA.) Hey, Big 'Un, a pack of my cigarettes and uh, these Cheetos.

VERA. The name is Vera. Vera Lisso, not Big 'Un. We've been through this a few hundred times.

(VERA moves behind the counter to get JUANITA's cigarettes.)

JUANITA. Big 'Un suits you better. *(To other ladies.)* The Basque people make a cheese out of raw milk that is aged in a cave for four or five months.

(JUANITA pays VERA, who places her change on the counter.)

MRS. BARNES. How do you know that, Juanita?

JUANITA. I forget. *(Pushes change back at* **VERA.***)* Keep the change, Big 'Un.

VERA. It's two pennies!

JUANITA. All yours. *(Back to ladies.)* It's ripened with mold, and they scrape the mold off before you eat it. And that's where the Basque people lost me!

    *(***JUANITA*** exits with her purchases.)*

VERA. The gates are down and the lights are flashing, but the train is not coming!

    (Lights out on The Corner Stop.)

Scene Fifteen

(Cast: **WARDELL, ODELL, G.W., JUANITA, LAVONDA, NOLETA, HARDY.***)*

(In darkness a rousing rendition by **WARDELL** *and the Bar Band of* [**"WILL THE CIRCLE BE UNBROKEN"**] *starts. Lights up on Bubba's Bar to reveal* **WARDELL** *on the bar stage, standing behind a microphone, on guitar,* **JUANITA** *on tambourine,* **ODELL** *blowing into a beer bottle and* **G.W.** *playing his legs with drumsticks, performing the song.* **HARDY** *stands by the bar, crutches by him, along with other available actors, now town folks. A big picture of* **PEGGY** *hangs behind the bar now. Lights up outside Bubba's as* **LAVONDA** *and* **NOLETA** *come rushing up.)*

LAVONDA. Come on, Noleta!

NOLETA. *(Adjusting her ponytail.)* Is my ponytail straight?

LAVONDA. Yes! Now behave yourself!

(Lights out outside Bubba's Bar as they enter. **NOLETA** *spots* **HARDY,** *at the bar. He motions her over.* **WARDELL** *spots* **LAVONDA.***)*

WARDELL. *(In microphone.)* Come sing with me, Vonie!

*(***LAVONDA** *joins the motley group on bar stage and sings in harmony with* **WARDELL** *in the microphone, smiles of love exchanged. As they sing,* **NOLETA** *and* **HARDY** *get cozy.)*

WARDELL, LAVONDA AND BAND. *(Singing.)*
WILL THE CIRCLE BE UNBROKEN
BY AND BY, LORD, BY AND BY
THERE'S A BETTER HOME A-WAITING

IN THE SKY, LORD, IN THE SKY.

WARDELL. Take that verse, Vonie.

LAVONDA. *(Singing.)*
I WAS STANDING BY MY WINDOW,
ON ONE COLD AND CLOUDY DAY
WHEN I SAW THAT HEARSE COME ROLLING
FOR TO CARRY MY MOTHER AWAY.

> *(**G.W.** notices **NOLETA** and **HARDY** and is not happy. **NOLETA** exchanges a glare with **G.W.**, then grabs **HARDY** and the couple start wildly making out. **G.W.** gets angrier and angrier during:)*

WARDELL, LAVONDA AND BAND. *(Singing.)*
WILL THE CIRCLE BE UNBROKEN
BY AND BY, LORD, BY AND BY
THERE'S A BETTER HOME A-WAITING
IN THE SKY, LORD, IN THE SKY.

> *(Slowing for the big finish.)*

THERE'S A BETTER HOME A-WAITING
IN THE SKY, LORD, IN THE SKY.

> *(The audience applauds as **NOLETA** and **HARDY** continue to kiss. **JUANITA** exits. **G.W.** sees red.)*

LAVONDA. *(Laughing.)* Thank y'all, oh, that was my mama's favorite hymn. That was just beautiful, Wardell.

> *(They step away from the microphone.)*

WARDELL. You know what's beautiful? You. Vonie, last night was real special for me.

LAVONDA. For me, too.

> *(**G.W.** suddenly throws down the drumsticks.)*

G.W.. That's it!

> (**G.W.** *waddles over at record speed to* **HARDY** *and* **NOLETA.**)

(Yelling.) Hey, you sumbitch!

> (**G.W.** *reaches* **HARDY** *and shoves him.*)

HARDY. What the hell?

NOLETA. Oh hey, G.W. I didn't see you standin' there.

G.W.. Get your goddamn hands offa her!

NOLETA. You have no claim to me! Our D-I-V-O-R-C-E became final seventeen years ago!

> (**LAVONDA, WARDELL, ODELL** *rush over to the confrontation, along with the others at the tribute.* **G.W.** *shoves* **HARDY** *again.* **HARDY** *stands, unmoved, towering over* **G.W.**)

LAVONDA. Oh, for cryin' out loud! Wardell, do something! They're ruinin' my Mama's tribute!

NOLETA. They're fightin' over me, LaVonda! Oh, they're fightin' over me!

> (**G.W.** *deliberately knocks over* **HARDY**'s *crutches that rest against the bar.*)

HARDY. Oh, you done it now, asshole!

> (**G.W.** *doubles his fist,* **ODELL** *getting behind him.*)

G.W.. It's on, you sumbitch!

> (**ODELL** *gives* **G.W.** *a shove towards* **HARDY.**)

ODELL. Go on, knock his teeth out, G.W.!

> (**G.W.** *punches* **HARDY** *in the jaw.* **HARDY** *doesn't even flinch.* **G.W.** *holds his hand.*)

Got 'im!

G.W.. *(In pain.)* Goddamn.

> *(**ODELL** pushes **G.W.** into **HARDY** again.*
> *Following should be overlaps.)*

ODELL. Come on, kick his ass!

WARDELL. Get the hell out of here, you nitwit! *(Mutters.)*
Quit eggin' 'em on.

LAVONDA. Shit! Do something!

WARDELL. They got this. Let 'em work it out.

LAVONDA. Y'all stop it!

> *(**ODELL** exits as **HARDY** pushes **G.W.** behind*
> *the bar and they wrestle. **HARDY** pulls off one*
> *of **G.W.**'s legs.)*

G.W.. Sumbitch took my leg!

> *(**HARDY** throws the leg over the bar. **G.W.** pulls*
> *himself up, grabs one of **HARDY**'s crutches*
> *to keep from falling. **NOLETA** rushes over to*
> ***LAVONDA** and grabs **G.W.**'s leg.)*

*(Pointing at **NOLETA**.)* Get that pyromaniac tramp
away from my leg!

> *(**HARDY** charges **G.W.** using one crutch, **G.W.***
> *not backing down with the other crutch.)*

HARDY. She ain't no tramp, and gimme back my crutch
right now! You gimme back –

> *(As **HARDY** goes for **G.W.** again, grabbing*
> *his other crutch, **WARDELL** pulls out his gun*
> *concealed in his Wranglers and shoots in the*
> *air. Silence.)*

WARDELL. Y'all oughta be ashamed of yourselves! We are trying to honor the life of a good woman here today, and y'all are ruining it! Noleta, you came in here just seekin' trouble. Now you get outta my bar and get yourself a room at the Galaxy Motel! And G.W., stop this damn nonsense! You forfeited every right you had in your marriage to Noleta.

NOLETA. That's right.

WARDELL. Peggy was the one you really loved buddy. You loved Peggy.

G.W.. *(On the verge of tears.)* I know.

WARDELL. Let's show 'er that tonight, huh?

G.W.. *(Now crying.)* Okay.

NOLETA. I'm sorry, Wardell. LaVonda, Hardy will give me a ride.

> (**NOLETA** *and* **HARDY** *exit.*)

LAVONDA. I'm sure he will. *(To* **G.W.***)* Now put your leg back on!

> (**LAVONDA** *walks over and hands* **G.W.** *his leg. Lights out on Bubba's bar.*)

Scene Sixteen

(Cast: **VERA, NURSE SAMPLE, MRS. BARNES, LATRELLE, SISSY, ROGER, TY, KYLE, JIMMY RAY, WILSON, BROTHER BOY.***)*

(Lights up church. A slow piano version of **["WILL THE CIRCLE BE UNBROKEN"]** *is being sung badly by* **VERA, NURSE SAMPLE** *and* **MRS. BARNES,** *all behind a pulpit.* **WILSON, GRETA** *and* **JIMMY RAY** *are already seated. Any cast ensemble and crew available to play church people are seated in rows of chairs or pews in front of the pulpit.)*

NURSE SAMPLE, VERA, & MRS. BARNES. *(Singing.)*
WILL THE CIRCLE BE UNBROKEN
BY AND BY LORD, BY AND BY

> *(***LATRELLE** *and* **SISSY** *come rushing in,* **SISSY** *smoking.)*

SISSY. Hurry up Latrelle, they've already started!

> *(***SISSY** *realizes she's still got a cigarette, takes one last drag, then throws it out the door, over* **LATRELLE***'s head.* **LATRELLE** *sees* **WILSON** *and* **GRETA.***)*

LATRELLE. Look who's here.

SISSY. Lordy, lordy.

NURSE SAMPLE, VERA & MRS. BARNES. *(Singing.)*
THERE'S A BETTER HOME A-WAITIN'
IN THE SKY LORD, IN THE SKY.

> *(Slowing for the big, horrible finish.)*

THERE'S A BETTER HOME A-WAITING
IN THE SKY, LORD, IN THE SKY.

(LATRELLE and SISSY sit as VERA and the ladies finish the song.)

VERA. Yes, brothers and sisters, let's keep our circle from being broken by sodomite sinners!

MRS. BARNES. Amen!

NURSE SAMPLE. And please forgive our appearance today. Roger, an avowed homosexual, has decided not to fix anybody's hair who believes in this good book. *(She lifts up her Bible.)* Amen!

(Lights up outside the church on ROGER when his name is mentioned by NURSE SAMPLE walking up to the church. He stops and listens on the steps.)

MRS. BARNES. Are y'all ready for some good old fashion preachin'?

CONGREGATION. Yes! Amen! We are!

Please welcome to Southside Baptist, our new pastor, my nephew... Jimmy Ray Brewton.

(JIMMY RAY takes the pulpit, the ladies take their seats.)

JIMMY RAY. Thank you for that beautiful testimony in song and for that warm welcome, ladies. Let's all grab our Bibles and turn to Leviticus, chapter eighteen, verse twenty-two.

(TY and KYLE come rushing up outside church, stopping when they see ROGER. Lights crossfade to church steps.)

TY. Roger?

ROGER. Ty?

(They hug.)

TY. Roger, this is my husband Kyle.

KYLE. Nice to meet you, Roger.

ROGER. And you. Lord, these people are not gonna know whether to be racist or homophobic.

TY. I'm sure they can do both. Did I miss anything?

ROGER. Nothing you haven't heard a hundred million times before. But that preacher is hot as fuck!

(They listen as lights crossfade to church.)

JIMMY RAY. *(Reading from Bible.)* "Thou shalt not lie with mankind, as with womankind: it is an abomination."

VERA. Amen, brother!

JIMMY RAY. You know, Satan was the first to ask for equal rights. Yeah, that's right. Flip over to Isaiah 14:14 where Lucifer proclaims, "I will be like the most high." Wanted to be equal with God. But Satan never got his equal rights, did he? No! No, he fell down to the bowels of hell. Just like the gays will.

(Lights crossfade to church steps.)

ROGER. I used to love this church.

KYLE. You know they're not all like this anymore.

ROGER. You can't swing a cat in this town without hitting a bigot.

TY. I remember. But you know, hearts and minds are changing. You question the creation, you question the Creator. You put a face on gay, Roger. And you did it here when nobody was doing that. You do realize you're my hero?

ROGER. Oh please. I'm nobody.

TY. That is so not true. *(To KYLE.)* When I was a little boy, I used to sit and watch Roger do Mama and Aunt

LaVonda and Aunt Sissy's hair, and I used to pretend that I was Roger from The Beehive! I ratted my doll Suzy Q's hair until she was bald. *(Back to* **ROGER.***)* You inspired me to accept all of me. So, thank you.

ROGER. *(Through emotion.)* You don't know what that means to me.

TY. We better get in there. Are you coming?

ROGER. Oh, hell no! I can hear the hate just fine from out here.

> *(Lights on church as* **TY** *and* **KYLE** *enter, the sermon roaring back to life. Lights dim on* **ROGER**, *who has had enough and exits.* **TY** *and* **KYLE** *greet* **SISSY** *and* **LATRELLE** *and stand behind them.)*

JIMMY RAY. But you are here tonight because you believe in the sanctity of marriage. You believe in one man, one woman. You believe in this good book. *(Lifts up the Bible.)* You believe that Winters, Texas can be protected from the outside evils and the lifestyles of the sodomites! You see, the Supreme Court is not the supreme being. And I thank the good Lord for Texas. It starts at the top with our god-fearing new Governor... Greg Abbott and our Attorney General, also a friend of Jesus, Ken Paxton... and trickles right down to Runnels County. I talked to Gail Wade, our County Clerk, today and Tinky Walker, our Justice of the Peace.

> *(***JIMMY RAY*** indicates someone in the audience.* **SISSY** *looks back at them,* **LATRELLE** *getting more and more agitated as the sermon continues.)*

Good Christian warriors! They have assured me that exercising their religious freedom will no longer allow same sex couples to get married in Runnels County. You know what that means? Gays can't get married in the church! Gays can't get married at the courthouse! No place to get married, nobody to marry them! We have shut out the sodomites... and those wretched pedophiles will no longer persecute good God-fearing Christians. And tonight, I proclaim that Runnels County be a sanctuary county, free of gay marriage. We have stopped equality!

LATRELLE. *(Standing.)* Oh, no you haven't!

> *(The* CONGREGATION *turns, shocked by* LATRELLE'*s outburst.)*

JIMMY RAY. Sister, do you have something to say?

LATRELLE. *(Rises.)* Oh yes, Brother, I have plenty to say!

JIMMY RAY. Well, alright, let's hear what the good sister has to say.

> *(*LATRELLE *starts towards the pulpit,* SISSY *now rising as the* CONGREGATION *whispers.)*

LATRELLE. Come on, Sissy! Grab your Bible.

> *(They head towards the pulpit,* SISSY *waving her Bible.)*

SISSY. I got it!

> *(They reach the pulpit.* JIMMY RAY *steps aside as* LATRELLE *takes the pulpit,* SISSY *standing meekly by her.* LATRELLE *looks at the* CONGREGATION, *taking them in, then speaks, tentatively at first, but gaining confidence as she goes.)*

LATRELLE. My son is gay. And my sweet Aunt Sissy has been doing research on his behalf.

SISSY. Read the Bible from cover to cover.

LATRELLE. Sissy, what does Jesus say about homosexuality?

SISSY. Not one blessed word.

JIMMY RAY. That is not true!

SISSY. *(Snaps.)* Yes, it is!

JIMMY RAY. First Corinthians –

SISSY. That was Paul, not Jesus!

LATRELLE. *(Turns to him.)* If you have a theology degree, get it right! Jesus said nothing.

SISSY. *(To JIMMY RAY.)* Nothing! *(To CONGREGATION.)* Do you believe in all the Bible?

JIMMY RAY. Of course we do.

CONGREGATION. *(Overlap.)* Yes. Of course. Amen!

SISSY. Then why do you eat bacon? Deuteronomy 14:8, "And the swine, it is unclean unto you: ye shall not eat their flesh." The Bible says to all of us who eat bacon and pig's feet and pork chops and Dorito sausage casserole...that eatin' pork is wrong. But bacon is *good*, and we eat it 'cause this scripture don't make one lick of sense.

MRS. BARNES. That's the Old Testament. Jesus gave us a new law.

VERA. That includes me getting to eat bacon!

LATRELLE. Yet Vera, you were the first to scream "Amen" when the pastor read from the Old Testament, "Thou shalt not lie with mankind, as with womankind: it is an abomination."

KYLE. *(Whispering to TY.)* I have never lied with a woman once the way I lie with you, baby!

TY. *(Suppressing laughter.)* Stop.

LATRELLE. And the New Testament certainly tells women to be silent – and Vera, Mrs. Barnes, Nurse Sample, y'all never shut up!

SISSY. And Tinky, Gail, y'all issued three of my five wedding licenses and adultery is riddled all over both Testaments and says that adulterers should be stoned to death.

JIMMY RAY. I demand that you sit down right now and stop hijacking this service with your own agenda and support for this deviant, perverted behavior!

> (**LATRELLE** *wheels on* **JIMMY RAY,** *getting right in his face.*)

LATRELLE. I am not done! And unless you want a scene that involves kicking and screaming and scratching and clawing out some eyeballs and taking that Bible and beating you with it the way you beat people with it, then I would advise you to back off and regroup until I am done!

KYLE. *(Yelling out.)* Go, Latrelle!

SISSY. Latrelle's not normally this violent, but you have set her off, so just... *(Shoos him with her hands.)*

LATRELLE. Sissy, please read the scripture that I have chosen for my sermon.

> (**SISSY** *flips through her Bible.*)

SISSY. *(Reading.)* John 4:7, "Dear friends, let us love one another."

> (*Long pause.* **SISSY** *and* **LATRELLE** *look at the silent* **CONGREGATION.**)

LATRELLE. That's all. Simple. Just love. Says it all, doesn't it? My son, Ty, and his husband, Kyle, have now gotten married in every state except Texas.

SISSY. Gay activists they're called. They did it as a publicity thing for Ty's job which helps the gays.

LATRELLE. *(Looks at* **WILSON.***)* And we taught our son to fight for what is right. And I'm ashamed to say that I always found a reason not to attend their weddings. *(To* **TY** *and* **KYLE.***)* And I'm sorry, Ty. Kyle, truly sorry. I guess, because deep down, it just went against everything I was taught right here at Southside Baptist. *(Emotional.)* But then, something happened that changed my heart. Ty and Kyle... they're going to be daddies. And you, Reverend Brewton just preached that gays should not be parents. That they are pedophiles.

JIMMY RAY. That is the truth!

LATRELLE. Liar! It is so far from it. I know my boy, he is not that. He is not capable. He has a good heart. Pure. *(Looks at* **WILSON.***)* And you know him too, Wilson. And I know you love him. *(To* **CONGREGATION.***)* All those sermons like this one tonight, calling my beautiful son and his beautiful husband pedophiles...abominations... sinners...well, those sermons are wrong.

JIMMY RAY. I preach the word of God!

LATRELLE. No, you cherry pick what serves your agenda! Sissy has proven that tonight. *(To* **CONGREGATION,** *emotional.)* And we must stop villainizing our children. Telling them that they are not worthy of God's love. Because they are. Just as they are. And right now, just down the street at Bubba's Bar, they are celebrating the life of my Mama... who did not die from a tumor that was pressin' against the sexual part of her brain. I lied, okay? A real sin. To cover up the truth. But no more cover-ups. *(Deep breath.)* My son is gay. And I am proud of him. All of him. And so, I would like to turn my Mama's celebration of life into a celebration of love and end this hateful night led by this hateful person. So, I invite all of you to come with me, and with my Aunt Sissy, and with my son and son-in-law and my brother, Brother Boy.

> **(BROTHER BOY** *storms in the church in full Tammy Wynette drag.)*

BROTHER BOY. Well, I guess y'all didn't think I was gonna make it, did ya – bigots!? Come on, Latrelle! I gotta show to do!

>   (**BROTHER BOY** *turns and struts out of the church;* **LATRELLE** *and* **SISSY** *rush down after him. Lights out on church.*)

Scene Seventeen

(*Cast:* **LATRELLE, SISSY, LAVONDA, TY, KYLE, BROTHER BOY, ROGER, WARDELL, JUANITA, G.W., ODELL, WILSON, GRETA.**)

(*Lights up on Bubba's bar and music cue intro to a song in the style of Tammy Wynette's* **["WOMANHOOD"]** *as* **LATRELLE, SISSY, TY** *and* **KYLE** *filter in to join the bar celebration.* **LATRELLE** *stands back from the stage,* **SISSY** *and* **LAVONDA** *right up front.* **TY** *and* **KYLE** *find a place to enjoy the show.* **G.W.** *and* **ODELL** *are back on their stools,* **WARDELL** *behind the bar.* **ROGER** *stands on bar stage with microphone.*)

ROGER. Ladies and gentlemen, would you please help me welcome to the stage, the first lady of country music – Miss Tammy Wynette!

(**ROGER** *moves from the bar stage and the spotlight hits* **BROTHER BOY,** *still in Tammy Wynette drag as he enters taking the microphone from* **ROGER** *and walks onto the bar stage, lipsyncing. This time, his performance is perfect! He sings a verse and a chorus, all AD-LIB approval. Spotlight out as* **BROTHER BOY** *rushes off stage, followed by* **ROGER.**)

---

* A license to produce A VERY SORDID WEDDING does not include a performance license for "WOMANHOOD". The publisher and author suggest that the licensee contact ASCAP or BMI to ascertain the music publisher and contact such music publisher to license or acquire permission for performance of the song. If a license or permission is unattainable for "WOMANHOOD", the licensee may not use the song in A VERY SORDID WEDDING but should create an original composition in a similar style or use a similar song in the public domain. For further information, please see Music Use Note on page 3.

SISSY. What's he doin'?

LAVONDA. Oh, it's his new act. It's called "We Three Queens of Opry Are".

> (**WARDELL** *comes out from behind the bar, heads to* **LAVONDA**.)

WARDELL. Hey Vonie!

LAVONDA. Hey, Wardell!

WARDELL. Just wanted to make sure my girl was okay. *(She smiles and nods.)* Brought you this.

> *(He gives her a beer.)*

LAVONDA. I am now. *(Takes beer.)* Thank you, baby.

WARDELL. Baby. I like that.

SISSY. Awwww.

WARDELL. Well... I gotta get back to the bar.

LAVONDA. Okay, I'll see you later. *(Sweetly, looks around.)* Thanks for all this.

> *(They kiss.)*

SISSY. Awwww.

BROTHER BOY. *(Off stage.)* Fix my wig, Roger! Hurry!!! Hurry!!!

> (**ROGER** *rushes in and onto the stage with a microphone.*)

ROGER. Please make welcome to the stage the queen of country music – Loretta Lynn!

(*Music cue intro in the style of Loretta Lynn's*
**["YOU AIN'T WOMAN ENOUGH (TO TAKE
MY MAN)"]** *during* **ROGER***'s introduction.*)

SISSY. Is he, is he bringin' back Loretta?

LAVONDA. He sure is!

(**ROGER** *rushes off the bar stage, handing the
microphone to* **BROTHER BOY** *spotlight hits*
BROTHER BOY, *now in full Loretta wig and a
big white ballgown.*)

SISSY. Spittin' image!

LAVONDA. Sissy Spacek, eat your heart out!

(**BROTHER BOY** *performs as Loretta to
perfection.*)

SISSY. (*Overlap.*) Sang it, Loretta!

(**WILSON** *walks into the bar with* **GRETA.**
TY *sees them and whispers something to*
LATRELLE, *who turns and sees them.* **KYLE**
also clocks them, puts his arm around **TY,** *as
if he's protecting him.* **WILSON** *spots* **TY** *and*
KYLE. *A moment as their eyes meet.* **TY** *quickly
looks away, back to watching* **BROTHER BOY.**)

Aw, this brings back memories, don't it?

---

* A license to produce A VERY SORDID WEDDING does not include a
performance license for "YOU AIN'T WOMAN ENOUGH (TO TAKE
MY MAN)". The publisher and author suggest that the licensee contact
ASCAP or BMI to ascertain the music publisher and contact such music
publisher to license or acquire permission for performance of the song.
If a license or permission is unattainable for "YOU AIN'T WOMAN
ENOUGH (TO TAKE MY MAN)", the licensee may not use the song in
A VERY SORDID WEDDING but should create an original composition
in a similar style or use a similar song in the public domain. For further
information, please see Music Use Note on page 3.

(Spotlight out as **BROTHER BOY** *finishes a verse and chorus rushes offstage again,* **ROGER** *right behind.* **WILSON** *walks over to* **TY**. **LATRELLE** *turns and watches as* **WILSON** *approaches* **TY** *from behind. He puts his hand on* **TY**'s *shoulder.)*

WILSON. Son –

*(**TY** flinches, looks to **KYLE**. **KYLE** gives him an affirming nod and **TY** turns around.)*

I've never understood you, Ty... and maybe I've never really tried...but... I heard what your Mother had to say tonight... and... I want to be a better father. So, if you'll let me, I'd like to try to be in your life again.

TY. I'd like that. And I'd like our children to know their grandpa.

*(**WILSON** grabs **TY** and hugs him, long and hard. **LATRELLE** watches, her eyes fill with tears. **TY** succumbs to the hug and hugs **WILSON** back.)*

WILSON. It's good to see you happy, son.

(They break the emotional hug.)

I'd like you to meet my wife... Greta.

TY. Greta... it's nice to meet you.

GRETA. You too, Ty.

TY. And I would like you to meet my husband.

*(**KYLE** steps up, extends his hand.)*

KYLE. I'm Kyle.

*(**WILSON** shakes **KYLE**'s hand.)*

WILSON. Hello, Kyle. I'm looking forward to getting to know you.

> (**ROGER** *rushes back on stage with the microphone.*)

ROGER. Please make welcome to Bubba's Bar, the legend herself – Miss Dolly Parton!

> (*Music cue intro in the style of Dolly Parton's* [**"JUST BECAUSE I'M A WOMAN"**] *'begins during* **ROGER***'s introduction.* **ROGER** *hands off the microphone and the spotlight hits* **BROTHER BOY** *as he returns to the stage in a Dolly wig and a low-cut short white dress.* **SISSY** *squeals.*)

BROTHER BOY. If I had these titties, I'd rule the world.

SISSY. Is that who I think it is?

LAVONDA. Yes, yes it's Dolly!

SISSY. Look at them titties! Oh my word!

> (**BROTHER BOY** *performs with confidence and perfection.* **JUANITA** *staggers in studies* **BROTHER BOY** *who sings right to her.*)

JUANITA. I am so confused.

> (**LAVONDA** *pulls out a wad of bills, then turns and finds* **LATRELLE.***)

---

* A license to produce A VERY SORDID WEDDING does not include a performance license for "JUST BECAUSE I'M A WOMAN". The publisher and author suggest that the licensee contact ASCAP or BMI to ascertain the music publisher and contact such music publisher to license or acquire permission for performance of the song. If a license or permission is unattainable for "JUST BECAUSE I'M A WOMAN", the licensee may not use the song in A VERY SORDID WEDDING but should create an original composition in a similar style or use a similar song in the public domain. For further information, please see Music Use Note on page 3.

LAVONDA.   *(Yelling.)* Latrelle, Latrelle! Come here! Latrelle, Latrelle, come here!

> (**LATRELLE** *looks confused as she goes over to* **LAVONDA** *and* **SISSY**.)

SISSY. Give me one!

> (**LAVONDA** *gives* **SISSY** *a couple of dollar bills.* **SISSY** *giggles as she tips* **BROTHER BOY**, *gingerly placing the bills between his fake breasts.* **LAVONDA** *does the same, then* **LAVONDA** *hands* **LATRELLE** *a dollar bill.*)

LAVONDA. Tip him! Put it down his bosom. Come on, come on. Take a dollar, put it down his bosom!

> (**LATRELLE** *takes the dollar, laughs as she figures out how to tip* **BROTHER BOY**.)

LATRELLE. Oh!

LAVONDA. That's it! You did it!

> (**TY** *steps up and shows how it's really done, holding a stack of bills and handing them over one by one as* **BROTHER BOY** *accepts them. Then* **TY** *motorboats the titties, laughs and hugs* **BROTHER BOY**. **LATRELLE** *watches the rest of the show with* **SISSY** *and* **LAVONDA** *as* **BROTHER BOY** *brings it on home. The crowd goes crazy with applause and appreciation, most having just witnessed their first drag show.*)

BROTHER BOY. Ah! Thank yewwww! Thank you so much!

> (*Spotlight out as* **LAVONDA**, **SISSY** *and* **LATRELLE** *rush the stage, hugging and greeting* **BROTHER BOY**.)

LAVONDA. You were so great!

SISSY. Awww.

LATRELLE. Just amazing.

> (**SISSY** *fixes on the fake breasts, presses them.*)

SISSY. *(Giggles.)* Them titties!

> *(They all hug, all together again, the picture of* **PEGGY** *looking over at them. Lights out on Bubba's Bar.)*

Scene Eighteen

(Cast: **ROGER, WILSON, GRETA, HARDY, WARDELL, ODELL, G.W., SISSY, LATRELLE, NOLETA, BROTHER BOY, JUANITA, LAVONDA, TY, KYLE, CREW MEMBERS.***)*

(Lights up on Bubba's Bar as stage crew, now in costumes, set up for the wedding. **ROGER** *enters, looks around, starts barking out orders as the wedding set is assembled: chairs with yellow bows, an arch with yellow roses on the bar stage, a boombox, perhaps some other yellow décor and a wedding cake.)*

ROGER. We still have lots to do, gang. *(To* **CREW MEMBER.***)* Sweetie, grab that boom box that's right behind the bar and put it on that side.

> *(The* **CREW MEMBER** *produces the boombox, which should look like an ill-fated gay craft project.)*

Good, good. *(To* **CREW MEMBER.***)* And you! I saw that look of judgment. *(Re: boombox.)* Yes, it's a little busy, but that's what happens when you're high on mushrooms and get crafty while listening to Sylvester's "You Make Me Feel (Mighty Real)". You have no idea who that is, do you? Gay history, darlin', gay history!

> *(***ROGER** *is now adjusting the yellow rose-filled arch on the bar stage. As he fiddles with the decorations, the* **CREW** *brings in the chairs.)*

Oh good, chairs! Two by two, just like all the straight animals in Noah's ark. Push those two back a little and make sure the bows are straight.

(ROGER rushes over and helps get the chairs where he wants them. A CREW MEMBER enters with a wedding cake with lots of yellow roses.)

Oh good, the wedding cake. *(Points to empty side of bar.)* Right over there, precious. *(Looks around, satisfied.)* Okay, great job. Run along now!

(He shoos the CREW out, then looks around, chokes up.)

Who'da ever thought this day would ever get here? Right here in Winters, Texas! *(Starts to cry.)* Oh Lord, save the tears! Not yet, not yet.

(ROGER opens the door.)

Welcome! Please come in and be seated everybody!

(ROGER ushers in WILSON and GRETA, followed by HARDY, maybe one or more available cast or CREW MEMBERS made to represent townspeople.)

There is no bride and groom side, y'all... you'll see why shortly. Just sit anywhere!

(GRETA starts to sit on the front row.)

Not there. That's my seat.

(She and WILSON sit on the second row. ROGER goes and hits the play button on the boombox. A country version of Pachelbel's [CANON IN D] begins to play.*)

---

* A license to produce A VERY SORDID WEDDING does not include a performance license for any third-party or copyrighted music. Licensees should create an original composition or use music in the public domain. For further information, please see Music Use Note on page 3.

(Emotional.) Well, fuck me runnin', the tears are flowing again. *(Calls offstage.)* Okay, boys, it's time. Get on out here!

> *(Dim lights up in the theatre audience, now part of the wedding.* **ROGER** *takes his seat as* **ODELL** *and* **G.W.** *walk onto stage with* **WARDELL,** *the groom. They are all dressed in their version of wedding attire,* **WARDELL** *in a western jacket and Wranglers. They position themselves on the groom's side of the arch. Lights up audience aisle as* **SISSY** *walks it, then up the stairs, into Bubba's Bar. She's our first bridesmaid, dressed in a yellow dress, the design influenced by* **LAVONDA's** *iconic ruffled, signature Mexican-style yellow blouse. She carries her purse and a yellow rose/baby's breath bouquet.* **SISSY** *smiles, overcome with emotion as she sees the décor,* **WARDELL** *and the groomsmen. She waves at* **WARDELL.** *Note: If theatre cannot accommodate actors in the audience, processional can be on the stage.)*

SISSY. Awww. *(As she passes* **ROGER.***)* You done a real good job, Roger. *(Nods to* **WILSON.***)* Wilson.

> *(***SISSY** *continues on and takes her place on the bride's side as* **LATRELLE** *appears in the aisle, dressed exactly like* **SISSY.** *She walks down the aisle, not happy about her dress, up the stairs, into Bubba's Bar. She shoots* **GRETA** *a dirty look as she passes her and* **WILSON.** *Then* **BROTHER BOY** *appears in the audience aisle, in his Tammy wig, perhaps bigger now, dressed just like* **LATRELLE** *and* **SISSY.** *He walks down the aisle, up the stairs, into Bubba's, pauses by* **ROGER.***)*

BROTHER BOY. *(Whispers.)* I do not want to steal the bride's thunder. Is my hair too big?

ROGER. Too big? What does that even mean?

BROTHER BOY. *(Smacks* **ROGER**, *playfully flirting.)* Oh!

> *(***BROTHER BOY*** *continues on and takes his place by* ***LATRELLE*** *and* ***SISSY***. ***NOLETA*** *follows, walks down the aisle in an identical dress, the maid of honor. She enters the bar and as she passes* ***HARDY***, *he reaches up and pinches her ass.)*

NOLETA. Oh, stop that! But not any time soon.

> *(***NOLETA*** *takes her place by* ***SISSY***.*)*

LATRELLE. I feel like Big Bird!

NOLETA. *(Adjusting her dress.)* I think this one can be repeated.

> *(Suddenly everybody reacts as* ***JUANITA*** *appears, walking down the audience aisle, dressed in her peach top and denim skirt. She has a basket of yellow rose petals in one hand, a bottle of beer in the other, a cigarette dangling from her lips. She drunkenly places her beer in the basket, then starts tossing the rose petals rather wildly at audience members.)*

LATRELLE. What is she doing?

SISSY. Looks like she's taken it upon herself to be the flower girl.

LATRELLE. She's ruining the wedding!

WARDELL. Naw, it's befitting.

(JUANITA *arrives at* GRETA *and* WILSON *and starts pelting* GRETA *with the remaining petals.*)

GRETA. Ahhhh! Wha... what are you doing? Ah! Seriously?

(JUANITA *smacks* ROGER *on the arm.*)

JUANITA. Scooch over, shug.

(ROGER, *irritated, gets up, moves down.*)

ROGER. What the fuck?!

(JUANITA *grabs her beer, takes a swig, sits, then loudly turns around to* GRETA *as she settles in her seat.*)

JUANITA. The royal family is falling apart because of inbreeding.

([**"BRIDAL CHORUS – HERE COMES THE BRIDE"**] *blasts and* LAVONDA *appears in the audience aisle. Her wedding gown is the same as the bridesmaid gowns, but a darker yellow, with flowers and ruffles on it.* TY, *in a suit, meets her to walk her down the aisle.*)

ROGER. Stand up, y'all!

(*Everybody does as* TY *and* LAVONDA *walk down the aisle.*)

LAVONDA. Oh, pinch me so I'll know this is really happening. (TY *does.*) Ouch! Yeah, this is really happening.

JUANITA. (*Confused.*) Who is that?

ROGER. The bride! LaVonda Dupree!

JUANITA. Doesn't ring a bell.

(WARDELL *watches* LAVONDA, *getting emotional.* G.W. *starts crying loudly as he shifts his gaze to* **NOLETA,** *who gives him dirty looks.* **ODELL** *squeezes* **WARDELL***'s shoulder.)*

ODELL. You found love, Bubba.

WARDELL. *(Still fixed on* **LAVONDA.***)* Yeah. Yeah, I did.

*(***TY** *and* **LAVONDA** *walk up the stairs, into Bubba's Bar and reach the arch. They turn to face the audience.* **TY** *indicates for all to be seated.)*

LAVONDA. Surprise everybody! It's gonna be a double wedding! Runnels County is now a sanctuary of love and we are having our first gay wedding! Fuck yeah! Get on out here, Kyle!

*(***KYLE** *enters also wearing a suit, and joins the wedding party, standing by* **TY.***)*

We're gonna have to wait a little longer, Wardell, because I'm going to officiate for the boys! We both got ordained on the damn internet!

WARDELL. I been waiting almost my whole life for this moment! What's a few more minutes?

SISSY. Awwwww.

G.W.. *(Crying louder, to* **NOLETA.***)* I'm so sorry I ever hurt you.

LAVONDA. Oh, hush up your bawlin', G.W.! This ain't about you!

NOLETA. That's right.

(Gives a little wave to **HARDY** *who waves back.)*

G.W.. Okay.

LAVONDA. *(Deep breath, begins officiating.)* We are here today to celebrate love. All love! Y'all, I'm about to wet myself I'm so giddy!

TY. *(Joking.)* Please don't.

LAVONDA. *(Serious.)* But really, who woulda ever thought we could have a gay wedding right here in the state of Texas? In Runnells County! In Winters fuckin' Texas! Tinky! Gail! Go suck on a dishrag!

ROGER. On a dishrag, bitches!

TY. *(To* **KYLE.***)* I told you to prepare yourself.

KYLE. Oh, I am ready, baby!

LAVONDA. Sissy, will you read that scripture we talked about?

> *(***SISSY** *pulls her Bible out of her purse, opens it.)*

SISSY. I sure will. Got it marked to the right place. *(She opens the Bible, steps forward and reads.)* First Corinthians 13:4-7. "Love is patient, love is kind. It does not envy, it does not boast, it is not proud. *(Looks up, with conviction.)* It does not dishonor others.

> *(The audience claps.* **SISSY** *takes a little bow, then returns to her place.)*

LAVONDA. I think that scripture fits both of us couples. Because Wardell, lord have mercy, cowboy, we been waiting a lifetime for this.

WARDELL. Damn right, we have.

LAVONDA. And Ty... and Kyle... *(Chokes up.)* I'm sorry... but I cannot even imagine the patience and the unkindness that you have had to endure because certain people are close-minded asswipes! *(Directly to* **WILSON** *and* **GRETA.***)* So... if you are here and you can't see the love that's here today fillin' up our hearts and this room, then something is wrong with you! Can I get an amen?

ALL. Amen!

ROGER. A-fuckin'-men!

JUANITA. Amen. Praise Jesus!

KYLE. *(To* **TY.***)* Best wedding yet!

LAVONDA. And y'all know that part in weddings where they ask that if anybody objects to speak now or forever hold your peace? Well, I'm not going to do that. Nope, I'm not going to! I'm just going to say –

> *(She flies off the bar stage and addresses the theatre audience, breaking the fourth wall.)*

if you have a problem with any of this – get up and get your bigoted asses out of here!

KYLE. Preach, Sister LaVonda!

LAVONDA. *(Preaching.)* You need to leave and don't let the door hit ya where the good Lord split ya! Get the hell right out of fuckin' Dodge! Now! *(Stares at the audience.)* Okay, good. Looks like all the right folks are finally in the same place here in Winters. The ones who are supposed to be here. *(Then sweetly.)* Ty, baby, favorite nephew of mine... *(Chokes up.)* I just want you to live your happy life with this beautiful man that you love. And to see your Mama here... And now your Daddy... *(Re:* **GRETA.***)* And that 'un. Well, it is indeed a special day. And Kyle, whether you like it or not, you are now part of our crazy family.

KYLE. I admit I'm a little scared, but thoroughly entertained.

LAVONDA. So it's time. You love birds join hands and say your vows, because me and Wardell aren't getting any younger.

(TY *and* KYLE *join hands.*)

TY. Well... since this is our fiftieth time to get married, I think we'll just make ours short and sweet. In my home state of Texas, I take you, Kyle Coleman, to be my lawfully wedded husband. Again.

KYLE. But... the difference is... this time, we finally have family here with us.

BROTHER BOY. *(Emotional.)* I am so glad I wore water-proof mascara.

> (SISSY *hands him a tissue, then one to* LATRELLE *and* NOLETA.)

KYLE. *(Turns to* LATRELLE.*)* Family love. There's nothing like it. And I thank you... *(Then turns to* WILSON.*)* ... and you... for raising the most exceptional man I've ever met, who is going to love our beautiful children just like he loves me.

LATRELLE. *(Through tears.)* Welcome to the family, Kyle.

KYLE. Thank you. *(Turns back to* TY.*)* I love you, husband.

TY. And I love you, husband.

BROTHER BOY. *(More emotional.)* And the flood-gates have officially opened.

> (NOLETA *blows her nose with the tissue* SISSY *gave her.*)

TY. *(To* LAVONDA *and* WARDELL.*)* And now, for the patiently waiting, it's your turn.

LAVONDA. Hold on! Y'all've made me a blubbering fuckin' mess.

> (NOLETA *rushes over and hands* LAVONDA *her used tissue.*)

NOLETA. Maid of Honor. At your service.

LAVONDA. *(Deep breath.)* Okay, I'm ready.

> *(**KYLE** steps back and **TY** steps up, taking **LAVONDA**'s place as the officiant. **WARDELL** and **LAVONDA** position themselves in front of **TY**.)*

TY. Aunt LaVonda and Wardell. It makes me so happy to see that you have reclaimed your love for each other. You are certainly living proof that love is patient and beautiful for all ages, colors, genders... and all levels of crazy! So... shall we just get to it?

LAVONDA. Yes! Yes! We shall!

TY. Wardell, do you take my awesome, audacious Aunt LaVonda to be your lawfully wedded wife?

WARDELL. Hell yeah, I do!

TY. And Aunt LaVonda, do you –?

LAVONDA. Oh, you can just skip all that other bullshit. 'Cause I do, too!

TY. Alright then! By the powers vested in me, I pronounce you husband and wife.

LAVONDA. And by the powers vested in me... off the internet... I pronounce y'all husband and husband!

NOLETA. Kiss! Kiss!

> *(And the couples do.)*

JUANITA. *(Staring at **TY** and **KYLE**.)* Princess Diana would approve.

SISSY. Awwww.

NOLETA. *(Excited.)* My first time to see a gay kiss and it was hot!

> *(**LAVONDA** turns to the crowd.)*

LAVONDA. Can y'all fuckin' believe it? Fuck, fuck, fuck, fuck, fuck, fuck, fuck!

> *(She tosses her bouquet and* **BROTHER BOY** *and* **NOLETA** *catch it simultaneously. Light effect simulating a camera flash. The wedding party freezes like a wedding picture.)*

> *(Blackout.)*

The End

NOTES FROM DEL SHORES
REGARDING MULTIPLE CASTINGS

When I decided to adapt *A Very Sordid Wedding* into a play, I decided that it would only work by keeping most of the characters. I always knew that multiple castings would be necessary for most productions. I did just that in casting and directing the world premiere. Below are the multiple castings in the Uptown Players production, along with some blocking and a rewrite that I hope will be useful for other productions.

The following multiple castings worked with quick changes and no changes in script or exits/entrances are needed:

Roger/Edna Jean/Cashier/*Anti-Equality Sister
Marty/*Nurse Sample/Tragic Drag Queen
Hardy/Peter
Peggy/Vera/Aunt Little Neecy/Hortense
*Actors played these roles in drag
Here are suggestions for double casting Odell/Jimmy Ray and Juanita/Mrs. Barnes.
Odell and Jimmy Ray

Act One, Scene Two: Odell was eliminated from the bar band so Jimmy Ray could roll out the church sign.

Act Two, Scene One: Odell was eliminated from bar band so Jimmy Ray could work on new signage.

Act Two, Scene Fifteen: Odell exited during the Hardy/G.W. fight (per Wardell's order) and quickly changed into Jimmy Ray for Scene Sixteen.

Act Two, Scene Seventeen: Odell entered and sat on his bar stool during Brother Boy's first number, once the actor has changed from Jimmy Ray.

Juanita and Mrs. Barnes
Exits and entrances have been written into the script to accommodate all the quick changes for this double casting except for:

Act Two, Scene Fourteen: Mrs. Barnes was eliminated from this scene, and the character of "Anti-Equality Sister" was added. The actor who played Roger, Edna Jean and Cashier also played Anti-Equality Sister. Here is the rewrite to accommodate this double casting:

ACT TWO

Scene Fourteen

(Cast: **VERA, NURSE SAMPLE, JUANITA, EXTRA ANTI-EQUALITY MEMBERS.***)*

(Lights up Corner Stop. **VERA** *sits on her stool, now in front of her counter. Her hair is a mess.* **NURSE SAMPLE** *works on her hair with an ancient* **ANTI-EQUALITY SISTER,** *also in desperate need of a hair appointment, working on* **NURSE SAMPLE***'s hair.* **OTHER ANTI-EQUALITY MEMBERS** *(if available) do the same. A chain gang of sorts.)*

VERA. Ladies, thank you for coming to our final Anti-Equality Committee meeting before the big revival tonight.

ANTI-EQUALITY SISTER. Hold still, sweetie. There's a hole in the back of your hair as big as Houston that I'm trying to cover.

NURSE SAMPLE. Ouch! I'm tender headed! Roger never hurts me! This is not working. We look like wet cats!

VERA. Roger is just a hateful-hearted homosexual who will pay for this by going straight to hell! *(Then sweetly.)* Sister Sample, please lead us in an opening word of prayer.

NURSE SAMPLE. Well, of course. Ladies. *(They stand and all join hands.)* Dear Heavenly Father, we gather here today in thy presence before our Anti-Equality Revival tonight. We pray for the soul of Sissy Hickey who now believes in equality. We pray for Latrelle Williamson who called our dear Vera a glutton. Let the church house be packed to the rafters, oh Lord!

ANTI-EQUALITY SISTER. Yes, Lord!

NURSE SAMPLE. Let sinners walk in that front door!

> (**JUANITA** *staggers in the store, takes in the scene.*)

JUANITA. What's going on here!?

NURSE SAMPLE. Juanita, hon, we're right in the middle of our final Anti-Equality committee meeting.

JUANITA. That doesn't sound right.

NURSE SAMPLE. Well, it is! Now, we would just love for you to come tonight as we stop equality from infiltrating Runnels County.

JUANITA. I have a conflict. There's something going on real important over at that bar that I sometimes frequent, uh, called uh... I forget.

VERA. Bubba's?

JUANITA. That would be the one.

NURSE SAMPLE. Might as well be called "The Den of Iniquity".

JUANITA. I think that one's over in New Orleans.

> (**JUANITA** *grabs a bag of Cheetos from the chip stand. Tosses them on the counter.*)

(To **VERA.***)* Hey, Big 'Un, a pack of my cigarettes and uh, these Cheetos.

VERA. The name is Vera. Vera Lisso, not Big 'Un. We've been through this a few hundred times.

> (**VERA** *moves behind the counter to get* **JUANITA***'s cigarettes.*)

JUANITA. Big 'Un suits you better. *(To other ladies.)* The Basque people make a cheese out of raw milk that is aged in a cave for four or five months.

> *(JUANITA pays VERA, who places her change on the counter.)*

NURSE SAMPLE. How do you know that, Juanita?

JUANITA. I forget. *(Pushes change back at VERA.)* Keep the change, Big 'Un.

VERA. It's two pennies!

JUANITA. All yours. *(Back to ladies.)* It's ripened with mold, and they scrape the mold off before you eat it. And that's where the Basque people lost me!

NURSE SAMPLE. *(Mutters.)* Trash.

> *(JUANITA exits with her purchases.)*

VERA. The gates are down and the lights are flashing, but the train is not coming!

> *(Lights out Corner Stop.)*

Sordid Lives

Margot Rose/Beverly Nero
Inspired by the play "Sordid Lives" by Del Shores

Sordid Lives

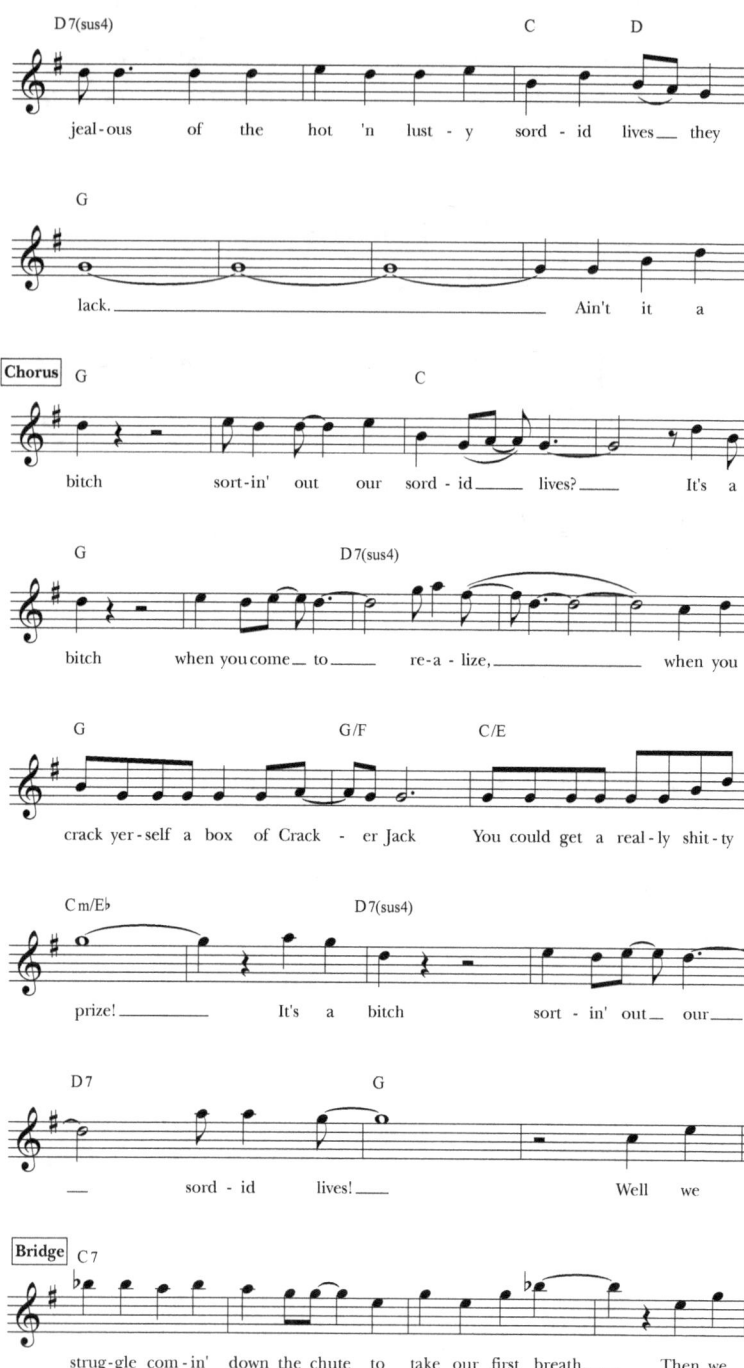

Sordid Lives

Margot Rose/Beverly Nero
Inspired by the play "Sordid Lives" by Del Shores

Sordid Lives

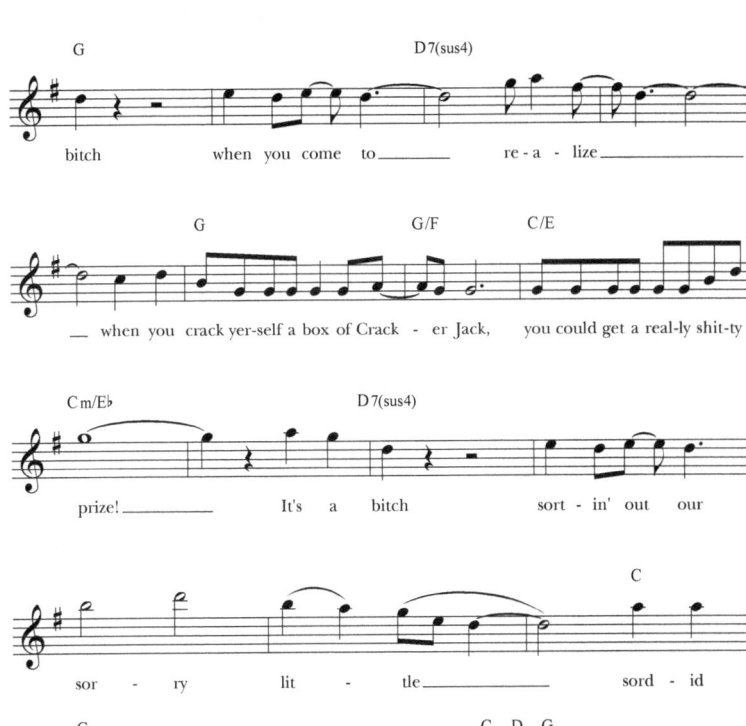

bitch   when you come to_____ re - a - lize_____

__ when you crack yer-self a box of Crack - er Jack,   you could get a real-ly shit-ty

prize!_____   It's   a   bitch   sort - in' out   our

sor - ry   lit - tle_____   sord - id

lives!"_____